# carp fishing

## on valium

# carp fishing

# on valium

AND OTHER TALES OF THE
STRANGER ROAD TRAVELED

# graham parker

ST. MARTIN'S PRESS ⚇ NEW YORK

www.stmartins.com

Design by Heidi D. Eriksen

Library of Congress Cataloging-in-Publication Data

Parker, Graham.
    Carp fishing on valium and other tales of the stranger road traveled : short stories / Graham Parker—1st ed.
        p. cm.
    Contents: The sheld-duck of the Basingstoke Canal — Aub — Chloroform — Bad nose — The evening before — Well well well — Me and the Stones — Carp fishing on Valium — Tinseltown, Morocco — The birdman of Cleveland.
    ISBN 0-312-26485-2
        1. Rock musicians — Ficiton.   2. Ornithologists — Fiction.   3. Middle aged men — Fiction.
    4. Comedians — Fiction.   I. Title.

PR6066.A578 C37 2000
823'.914–dc21

                                                              00-027855

First Edition: June 2000

10   9   8   7   6   5   4   3   2   1

# contents

# acknowledgments

Much praise to Tim Farrington and my literary agent, Laurie Fox, for their sharp editing skills, without which this work would have been a much sloppier affair. Thanks to John Cunningham at St. Martin's Press for taking this project on and digging the language of the English.

Enormous gratitude goes to my wife and very first editor, Jolie, who managed to decipher my hyperactive scrawl and get this collection into readable shape.

A very special mention goes to the late Marilyn Lipsius, who championed my writings before I even knew what double spacing meant.

Finally, I'd like to thank the many other people who read these stories and offered advice, little of which I took.

# carp fishing

## on valium

# the sheld-duck

## of the

## basingstoke canal

A t that time of the day—about eleven A.M. on a brilliant July morning—my grey plimsoles had wings on
them. They seemed to propel the rest of me forward as if
the compass and map that dictated my direction were se-
questered in their toe-caps, and not in the feverish spin of
my head. Bounding down Woodend Road with all the energy in my wiry thirteen-year-old frame crackling under my
skin, I flew across Blackdown Road and disappeared into
the woods like a hare.

I could never be happier. The summer holidays had
begun with a firm demarcation, a tingling, anticipatory
glee, but now, after a seemingly endless time, they promised to continue into eternity, as if each night of sleep was

a death to be resurrected from each sparkling morning. That's how it seemed, at any rate, until that dreaded, stomach-churning moment that arrived a week, two days, or the night before the blackest day of the year: the end of the summer holidays.

That moment, however, was eons away. Beyond the creosoted fence that bordered the far side of Blackdown Road, I arrived at the dung pit, my first stop of the day. I kicked around in the horse manure and turned over a few brandlings, those sticky red-striped worms that perch love so much. Then I thought of grass snake eggs, for I had found a lone papery specimen here last year. I couldn't remember what I'd done with it: traded it for marbles? a bird's egg? It seemed too much like a prize I would keep, place in an aquarium full of dung, and smuggle into the warmest spot in the house until it hatched. But racking my scatty, adrenaline-loaded brain, I recovered no recollection, and so, tapping the sweet-smelling cack from my shoes, I pelted off down the hill under the cathedral of elms, oaks, chestnuts, and pines.

As I bounced down the stony slope, casting fitful glances at the green horse pastures on either side, my mind sizzled with the choices that lay before me: I could keep going straight, over the sandy track at the bottom of the pastures and onward to the edge of the army married quarters in search of lizards on the heath. I could swing right at the track, head down to the back of the church, cross the road by the army museum, drop onto the tail end of Blackdown Road, and arrive at the canal under Kernley

Bridge to hunt newts, leeches, frogs, and snakes, keeping a sharp lookout for pike in the weedbeds. Or I could take a similar tack but veer left opposite the old museum and trudge up the road toward Pirbright and cut off into the gorse and broom thickets to the snake pit. On a day like this, lizards would be under the tins warming up, yet it was still cool enough for slow-worms and grass snakes — perhaps I might even spot an adder. All my options seemed good, any combination of choices was possible at this hour, and every scenario was likely to present the opportunity to pursue my natural history obsession of the moment: collecting birds' eggs.

There are some who may find the practice abhorrent; indeed, both of my bibles — *The Observer's Book of Birds* and *The Observer's Book of Birds' Eggs* — chastised against such temptation. But we "eggers," as we called ourselves, were sincere nature lovers, environmentalists before the word was invented. We loved wildlife in every form. (All right, I couldn't resist kicking the heads off of dandelions when bees settled upon them, and I once went through a bizarre and highly destructive phase of swinging a five-foot fiberglass fishing rod, tip-end in hand, cork butt to water, at baby pike as they hung motionless in the shallows of the canal waiting for prey. But bees are plentiful, and I quickly went through the pike-bashing stage, presumably a juvenile chemical imbalance, soon turning my hotheaded attentions to the destruction of property and the letting down of army officials' car tires — much less cruel practices.) Our policy was to take only one egg per nest from a clutch of four; we would never (well, very, very rarely, and only under extreme temptation, i.e., a particularly scarce specimen high in a tree or deep in a sand bank burrow) remove an egg from a nest of less than four.

It was the exquisite beauty of birds' eggs that evoked such avarice. They looked like pretty, egg-shaped china marbles. The sheer elegance and perfection of their colour, symmetry, and design made it impossible for us to keep our dirty hands from plucking one precious jewel, now and again, from the sweet warmth of those impossible little baskets. To have a dozen or so different specimens cushioned on a bed of sand in a shoe box was to be somehow closer to the secret of creation: that mysterious world of smells, sex, call and response, fight or flight, peck or be pecked. So badly did we hunger after knowledge of that world that we eggers would break a cardinal rule of nature lovers everywhere and take a thing that, if left alone, would one day become a life.

I hit the narrow sandy track at the bottom of the slope like a sprinter and in a split second made up my mind to cross it and seek out the even narrower trail on the other side, up through the pines toward the heathlands bordering the army barracks and married quarters. Perhaps while hunting for lizards I would chance upon a wheatear's nest with a second clutch. But as I was about to pelt through the overhanging leaves of a young, spindly oak, a face popped out of the foliage, red and watery-eyed with a mop of blond hair perched on top. It was Adrian, a big, flabby kid who had recently joined the junior school (which I had finally left this term, being a teenager and ready for the horrors of a modern secondary education).

Adrian was born in England but had moved with his army parents to Singapore, Germany, and finally Malta. I hadn't had time to really get to know him, but his nickname, "Beetroot," had made him instantly famous. His problem—a heady one for a kid—was severe blushing. Not just the usual kind triggered by the myriad embarrassments of childhood, but big heroic blushing, blushing on a giant scale. Massive scarlet sheets would run up his face from the neck at the slightest provocation. If a teacher called his name for no reason other than to check if he was present, Adrian's face would go off like a lightbulb and, if there was no repercussion, swiftly return to the whitest of white. If the poor devil had been caught in some hanky-panky and was hauled up for it, he'd be flashing like a brake light each time he was subjected to the scrutiny of his accuser's gaze. Anything could set a reaction off. Just yelling, "Hey, Beetroot, stop wanking!" would provoke eruptions of colour so fascinating that inevitably some other kid would hurl a personal comment Adrian's way just as he was recovering from the first, and off he'd go again.

I was not altogether happy about running into Adrian in the woods—not because I didn't like him (he was all right, though a little on the dull side), but because if there was going to be an expedition, I preferred to be the leader. I liked to devise the plan, designate the target, be the whip hand, and generally have some idea of the outcome. Bumping into someone unexpectedly always meant a quick shuffling of egos, and besides, I just felt like being alone that day. But worse than the explosively pigmented Adrian was the threat of another wild card. For there, bobbing up behind him through the lush oak leaves, was a second kid, a squatty, troll-faced little brute whom I did not recognize.

"Hey, hey, Brian!" chimed Beetroot, and there was no turning back.

"Hi, Beetroot," I said sheepishly. "Where ya goin'?"

"Nowhere," he answered. I felt a mild twinge of doom in my stomach. I didn't like the look of his friend at all. He wore lederhosen, for one thing, and his dark, bullety eyes regarded me with a disquieting air of threat.

"Do you know Angus?" asked Beetroot, pointing to his friend, who now stood on the path directly in front of me.

"Nah, 'e doesn't fuckin' know me," said Angus brusquely.

He didn't have a pure Scottish accent, but his name betrayed his roots. His father was probably some bolshie Scottish sergeant major with red bristles on his neck, recently stationed down south to whip some discipline into the northern squaddies who came to the Aldershot area in droves, escaping the unemployment in Birmingham, Sheffield, and Manchester. These lads arrived by the lorry load for the promise of a better life in the army with its plentiful bounty of fags, tarts, and cafes with milky tea and pinball machines.

I hated northerners on principle, and my experience with them hadn't changed that view. They were all as thick as two short planks as far as I could see, and their cock-o'-the-walk strutting made me want to puke. But this kid Angus had a mixed-up accent, part northern, part southern, which wasn't that uncommon in the kids of the local schools, most of whom were army brats who'd been dragged around from colony to colony, always awaiting "the boxes," as they called their permanently in-transit belongings.

Angus muscled up in front of me, hoisting his leather breeches and puffing up his big-boned chest like a budding sergeant major. He wore a tight khaki jacket and no shirt. His chest looked strong and greasy. I could tell he was the kind of twit who still played with toy soldiers and organized war games in sand pits. He stared me down from under one thick black eyebrow that ran above his dark eyes like an obscene caterpillar.

"What's your name, mate?" he demanded.

"Brian."

"Wanna fight?"

"I dunno . . . maybe," I stammered, feeling myself do a minor Beetroot imitation. My morning idyll had just evaporated under the gaze of this half-Scot lunatic, and a bag of nerves appeared where my stomach had been. I did not want to fight him — he looked as tough as a pound of nails to me — and tried to think of something quickly to defuse the situation. Like a big brown angel, the image of a bird flashed through my head.

"You from Scotland?" I blurted, hoping to distract him from the notion of fisticuffs.

"Yeah, so?"

"Ever see a golden eagle?"

"Lots of them!" he snapped, but of course he was lying.

There were definitely golden eagles in Scotland, but even I knew they weren't gliding over the towns and pecking in the gutters for stale chips. You had to know where to look. You had to go out to the remotest moorlands to see one, and I suspected that I had seen one more than Angus had.

It had been a year ago, and I was alone, heading toward the snake pit about a mile away from where I now stood. I happened to glance up at the blue sky and there, way, way up, was a massive bird in full flight, heading south. I knew immediately and instinctively that it had to be a golden eagle—nothing else could look like that. But how could it be? This was Surrey! I lived in the south of England, and golden eagles did not make their homes anywhere below the wild northern wastes of Scotland. But in the local paper the very next day, I read that a golden eagle had been spotted flying high in the sky over the Camberley area. Incredible! I'd actually seen it myself! All those birdie terms from *The Observer's Book of Birds* bounced around my head like pinballs: Rare migrant. Bird of passage. Rare visitor. Winter visitor. Vagrant. "Lost" was not a word used to describe anything in *The Observer's Book of Birds*, but I reckoned it would fit that eagle.

"Are you an egger?" asked Angus, successfully distracted from punch-up mode.

"Yeah, I am. I've got quite a few."

"You got a pied flycatcher's egg?"

"No," I enthused.

"Want one?"

"What, you know where a nest is?"

" 'Course I do, mate. I put an ammo box up in the woods an' there's a clutch of four left in there. I took one when there was five. But you mustn't tell anyone where it is, all right?"

"No, no. I wouldn't do that," I said honestly. If this kid could get me a pied flycatcher's egg, I'd not betray him. Such an egg would be a major addition to my collection. It would even beat my sand martin's egg that a long-armed kid named Denis had reached into a burrow for in the bank on the River Wey near Guildford. And my swan's egg was pretty special, too. I'd discovered it floating in a private pond I'd sneaked into earlier that year—quite a lucky find, seeing as you can't generally approach a swan's nest for fear of being pecked or wing-beaten to a pulp.

Family Muscicapidae.     Flycatchers
End April–September     Length 4 ¾ in.
*This small flycatcher is uncommon, but if seen is easily distinguished by its smart black and white plumage. It is a summer visitor. . . . The eggs are pale blue.*

9

I could visualize the picture in *The Observer's Book of Birds* and remember a few details of the text. There was the male in a black-and-white illustration, perched in a flowering dogwood with the dull, buff female a little further back, eyes beady for insects.

"Come on, then, let's go!" barked Angus. For once I didn't mind being a mere foot soldier, not if I was going to get a pale blue pied flycatcher's egg.

Adrian and I followed the brawny-legged and leathery-smelling Angus back up the slope toward my home, and off to the left into the pine copse close to the creosote-coated fence that divided the civilian village of Kernley from the army-owned woods of Blackdown. The three of us tramped under the dappled sun-shot needles.

In the darkness of a cluster of pines, surprisingly near the Catholic church, Angus stopped and peered up at the trunk of a tall Scots pine. There was the ammo box wedged between two of the lower branches. I'd converted ammo boxes myself with varying degrees of success, but could scarcely imagine something so exotic as a pied flycatcher, in such an unexotic locale, favouring one as a nest. You could expect a great tit or a blue tit or perhaps a tree sparrow—but a pied flycatcher?

Angus shinned up the tree, his lederhosen gripping the sappy bark like monkey skin. When he tapped the side of the nesting box, a small, undistinguished, buff-coloured bird shot from the hole and disappeared into the pines. The lad reached in and came out with a pale blue egg, which he held casually in one hand as he slid back down the trunk. He presented it to me nonchalantly, as if a pied flycatcher's egg were no great thing.

I held the perfect, warm ovoid in my hand, marveling at its uniform blueness. The male flycatcher was nowhere to be seen. We squatted nearby, hoping to catch a glimpse of the female again, but after five minutes gave up and walked over to the church to get a drink.

"Thanks, mate," I said as Angus sucked on the water from a tap that stuck out of the back of the old holy building.

"Told ya, didn't I?" he said, wiping his mouth on his khakis. "Pied flycatcher."

"Bloody great," I agreed. "I'm going home to blow it."

I drank deeply from the tap, which boasted the coolest, most delicious water I had ever tasted. I imagined it came from deep under the shady bowels of the church and not the village mains.

As we walked up Blackdown Road toward my house, Angus and Adrian decided to peel off into Key's Cafe for a cup of tea and a game on the machines. As they were about to enter the squaddie-filled dive, Angus turned to me casually and said, "I know where a sheld-duck nest is."

"A sheld-duck?!" I gasped. My brain flipped the pages of *The Observer's Book of Birds*. I would look it up when I got home, but vaguely remembered that sheld-duck are considered a marine species.

"Where?" I asked hopefully, knowing that bird habitats could be variable, especially in the imaginations of thirteen-year-old eggers.

"Down the canal," said Angus with complete authority.

Down the canal? My heart came into my mouth as the detailed illustration in the bird book appeared in my mind's eye. There was the handsome male sheld-duck, crouching in a low waddle — it was red-billed, pink-footed, black-headed, and decked out in all manner of flashy green-brown black and white glossiness. The bird was making for its burrow in a sand bank, the pale ocean behind it framed by stalks of yellow seagrass.

"Wanna go this afternoon? I know where it is — it might have laid by now," said Angus, leaning into the cafe door.

"Yeah!" I boomed.

"Whatcha got now?" asked my dad, squinting up at me from the cabbage patch, a white hanky, tied at the corners, perched on his head to keep the sun out.

"Pied flycatcher's egg," I answered, opening the back door and entering the kitchen.

"Flied piecatcher?" he queried, turning back to the cabbages, where he continued picking off the green caterpillars of the cabbage white butterfly, dropping them into a tin for drowning.

"Pied . . ." I answered, but didn't finish, anxious as I was to see this latest jewel placed with my collection.

In the quiet of my bedroom, I pulled the shoe box out of the drawer where it rested among my coin collection, stamp albums, and loose matchbox tops. I made a mental note to buy a new scrapbook next time I went to Aldershot; I needed to safeguard the matchbox tops before they got too crumpled with the constant opening and closing of the drawer.

Out in the back garden, I heard my mum and dad talking softly about the bloody caterpillars and slugs and other pests that shared the vegetables with us. My mum sat in a deck chair at the back of the garden on a small patch of lawn, flanked by a row of cabbages on the one side and rows of beans, lettuce, and cauliflowers on the other. She hadn't even heard me come in; she was going deaf, even back then.

I stared lovingly at the eggs sitting on their bed of sand in my box: the song thrush egg, turquoise blue, speckled with warm brown, but cracked from careless blowing (they were common and I could replace it at any time); the pale green mallard's egg, unmarked and big as a small chicken's egg; the coot, stony-buff and finely speckled with brown and black; the moorhen, creamy and pinkish, dotted with lavender-grey and dark brown. Beautiful! Then came the sand martin, the great tit, the pied wagtail, the blue tit, the long-tailed tit (I had suffered for this one, clawing through the thickest gorse bush, sustaining dozens of bloody scratches to reach the impossible oval dome made of moss, lichens, dog hairs, and spiderwebs), the chaffinch, the house sparrow, the tree sparrow, the bullfinch, the linnet, the starling, the jackdaw, the goldfinch, the greenfinch, the jay, the magpie, and finally, plucked from the pied wagtail's nest, the parasitic cuckoo's egg, looking for all the world like a blown-up version of its host's egg, but given away by its large size.

At the back of the drawer sat the white swan's egg cushioned in a bed of cotton wool. It was too big for the shoe box.

I extracted a fine sewing needle from the rummage of the drawer and went to the bathroom, where I carefully popped two tiny holes in both ends of the pied flycatcher's egg. I made one hole slightly larger by twisting the needle a little, and then I placed the smallest hole to my mouth and began to gently blow the viscous yolk into the sink. I could hear my parents murmuring outside, drowsy in the buzz of summer bees, their conversation punctuated every now and again by an explosive hacking cough from my father's smoker's lungs. A distant jackdaw cawed, and various tweetings from small birds spiked through the mélange of sweet homey sounds.

I tingled all over, happy as a sandboy, staring at the blue, blue flycatcher's egg as if it were the prize jewel in the Queen of England's crown. Back at the shoe box, I placed the egg gently between the streaky, dirty pink chaffinch's egg and the lightly speckled greenish-blue linnet's, which set it off nicely. I thought of the large, creamy-white sheld-duck's egg that might soon be mine. Experimenting with a space between the mallard's and the coot's, I concluded that yes, it would just fit in the crowded shoe box.

---

Beetroot, Angus, and I met by the old army museum that sat back off the road in a tangle of rhododendrons, pine trees, and mountain ash that grew feverishly a few hundred yards from the north bank of the Basingstoke Canal. The lads considered a quick tour of the museum but I put them off, having seen repeatedly the musty firearms, coats of arms, cruddy old uniforms, and the tin of chocolate presented to Queen Victoria that made up some of the museum's dusty relics.

"How far is it, Angus—this sheld-duck's nest?" It was past two when I'd left the village and I was anxious not to get caught miles away from home in the dark.

"Not too far," he answered. As we took off behind the museum, we were eyed suspiciously by the caretaker, who squinted through the dirty window of his office. Soon we reached the high bank of the canal and turned left, heading toward Pirbright and the numerous locks that dotted the old, disused waterway to Brookwood and beyond.

The towering elms, pines, oaks, silver birches, and beeches kept us cool. We moved at a fair clip, stopping occasionally to look down at the still, mirrorlike water of the canal. Whenever we stopped, the only sound we could hear, save birdsong, was the intense rustling of leaves as thousands—millions—of wood ants worked ceaselessly at their nests. The orange-and-black insects built huge piles of dead leaves and dirt, which we poked at with sticks, our eyes tearing up as the aggressive creatures flipped on their backs and sprayed the heavy air with formic acid from their rumps.

15

Before long, we arrived at the abandoned swimming pool, left to rot after an outbreak of polio after the war. We resisted a romp through the old, rotting changing cabins or a quick climb down the ladder into the marshy wastes that now grew on the floor of the ancient structure. Frogs were down there, newts, too. But this was a mission from which no distraction would detain me for long.

"So, when did you find the nest, Angus? And how far is it now?" I asked as we moved away from the canal, where the undergrowth had become too dense, and made our way up to the back of the sewage farm.

"It's . . . it's still quite a long way," he said vaguely.

Out in the full sun by the rotating arms of a sewage tank, we stopped for a breather. I immersed myself in the rich smell of sewage, blended with heady lilac and honeysuckle, and the annoying tang of Angus's lederhosen. Beetroot sat on a stump and absently scratched his balls.

"Stop wanking, Beetroot!" I scolded, triggering a rise of crimson across his face. Just then a sharp report rang out. We bolted back toward the thickets bordering the canal. It was the sewage farm attendant, who had shot at me once before. We peeked out from the bushes and saw the crazy old geezer pointing his pellet gun at us for another go. Finally he lowered the gun barrel and shouted, "Piss off, you little buggers!" Satisfied that we had gotten the message, he turned back to his old, dilapidated hut.

"Fuck off, you old bastard!" was my parting yell as we scrambled down the sandbank to a short towpath by the canal. Sandbanks! The perfect place for a sheld-duck nest.

NEST. *Of bents, moss and down, in a burrow, usually a rabbit's.*

EGGS. *6 to 12, creamy-white. May.*

FOOD. *Sand worms and hoppers, shellfish, snails, crus-taceans, seaweed.*

Well, it was a stretch, but we'd had a long, nasty winter, and birds that usually laid in April or May were still nesting, even now in July. And the book never mentioned a second clutch. Maybe they'd forgotten. Lots of birds had two clutches a year, and there were all kinds of freshwater shellfish in the canal and plenty of weeds for them to eat. Admittedly, it would be farfetched for a sheld-duck to be forty miles from the nearest coast, but I remained optimistic, convincing myself that where wildlife is concerned, there are always exceptions to the rules. Maybe a pair had just blown off course, like the golden eagle, and landed in the Basingstoke Canal and decided to nest there. Angus, after all, had procured the pied flycatcher's egg, and he did seem to know where he was going.

"Hey, Angus— sandbanks!" I said encouragingly.

"Nah, it's further than this," he mumbled, and on we trudged.

As the shadows lengthened, we came to the first lock. We paced gingerly across its massive crossbeams, one at a time, our arms out like tightrope walkers. This lock was low to the water, but the long series of locks that continued along the canal were twenty to thirty feet high and spanned the waterway, which was now reduced to a trickle,

17

except directly below the vast wooden structures. The giant rectangles had been cut in the days when barges navigated the canal, pulled by horses tramping the narrow sandy towpath. Now only a thin stream ran in the weed-choked, dried-up bed. The water accumulated at each lock mouth, finally dribbling down the concrete siding in a waterfall that rolled over the horizontal stonework and splashed into the foaming pools at the bottom.

The sun beat down on us as we stared into the first deep lock. I had a feeling that we were never going to have time to reach the sheld-duck's nest—not if we wanted to get home in time for tea. Maybe these army brats could stay out till all hours, but I'd been home late the last two nights after playing football, and I'd cop it if it happened again.

"It's a bit late," I said lamely. "Are we anywhere near?"

"Still quite a long way," replied Angus, swatting a mosquito from his eyebrow. "It might be dark before we get there. Maybe we should try it another time," he added with a dull resignation.

We decided to walk to the next lock and cross it back to the north side of the canal, and then head up to the bus stop near the barracks on the road to Pirbright. That would save hours and a long trudge home, retracing our steps. I followed the two boys along the towpath, which began to get muddy and overgrown, with occasional tree trunks wedged across it like natural turnstiles. Adrian lolloped along while Angus laboured moodily, his head a few degrees lower than when I'd first met him that morning. I knew he hadn't expected me to push it this far. I also knew by now that the sheld-duck was pure imagination, and in all probability, the pied flycatcher's egg was a hedge sparrow's. But I didn't confront Angus about it. We all used our heads to make life interesting—to get things going. There were unwritten codes about such things, codes that were never really examined. We wove our fantasy life into the fabric of nature, which made the whole world even more mysterious, more wild and unfathomable. Boredom was the only real enemy, and that could be vanquished with the slightest tweak of the imagination.

I left the two lads at the bottom of Blackdown Road where the bus had dropped us off. They went home to the married quarters. Realizing I had roughly an hour on my hands till the deeper dusk, I sprinted down Lake Road to a huge wild garden I would sometimes frequent. There, I knew, was a blackbird's nest, and by now I reckoned a nice fat clutch of brown-speckled green eggs would await—probably the third this year.

I crawled through the hole in the fence and made for the old orchard, peeking up at the house on the hill, which always appeared empty. I reached the kidney-shaped ornamental pond, long ignored, with its one massive goldfish—fully a two-pounder—that I had named Hercules. Crossing the low, narrow, crumbling stone bridge between the kidneys, I came to the dense rhododendron. Sure enough, as soon as I moved a branch, a drab female blackbird took to the air. I reached into the twiggy nest and felt four warm objects. With the deftness of a master pickpocket, I plucked one and brought it to the edge of the pond for inspection. Turning the egg in my fingers to examine its universe of brown speckles, I heard a thumping in the undergrowth nearby and dropped the egg on the concrete siding of the pool. Crouching low, my eyes flashed from egg to bushes until, suddenly, a head emerged from the low rhododendron leaves and the guileless face of a cross-breed Labrador popped out, tongue lolling and ready for play.

I stood quickly and shooed the animal—which I recognized as a harmless local from the village—and returned to the egg. Although it had landed on a patch of moss between the cracks of the crazy paving, it was still ruined, dented flat on the bottom and shattered lengthwise in three places.

The egg should have exploded, but instead the fragments of shell, which I now carefully picked away, were clinging to a gelatinous mass that lay beneath them. As I removed the final piece, I saw with sinking astonishment a perfect jelly sphere, inside which a tiny unborn fledgling kicked.

For as long as I dared, I studied that miraculous embryo as it twitched and kicked, its veins pumping blood to its clawlike winglets until a final beam of evening sun glanced through the foliage, illuminating a life that would never fly.

Back home, I went straight upstairs and took out the

shoe box and the swan's egg. I transported the lot up the back of the garden to the compost heap. My dad saw me march by, a fixed grimace on my face, but he resisted comment. One by one, I took those remarkable jewels out from their place in the sand and, with the side of my fist, crushed them on the compost heap.

With each sickening crunch, I cursed myself. When I had finished, I sat back on my haunches and stared, dull-eyed, at the dry pile for a long, long time.

D avy, Kevin "Bummer" Burroughs, and myself sat on the red plastic chairs at a white Formica table in the Woking Wimpy Bar, awaiting our usual orders of foamy, milky coffee and Wimpy burgers. The place was quiet on that Saturday morning; the lunch crowd hadn't come in yet and the other customers—two Pakistani house painters, a young couple with normal hair, and a greasy middle-aged woman who looked like she might have a screw loose—ignored the three of us as our burgers arrived and we tucked in with gusto. The softness of the buns and the melting beef washed down with sugary coffee were exquisite, and even though the rest of the clientele in the place that day were decidedly unfashionable, we knew that with the Wimpy and coffee ritual, our cropped Moddy Boy hair-cuts, our Levi's, white shirts, Doc Martens, and red braces, we were the height of smartness, and altogether hunky-dory.

I had come up to Woking on the Number 44 bus for a day's shopping, hanging out, and posing with my mates, on the hunt for a good pair of parallels or a small-collared shirt. We rarely actually bought anything, but I liked the peaceful bus ride through Pirbright, Brookwood, Knaphill, and the rest of the clean English suburbs, and what was there to do at home on a Saturday? At sixteen years old I could hardly go off into the woods anymore, and there was practically no one I wanted to be with in the village of Kernley. I was the only Moddy Boy in the whole place except Al and Stubs, and they were a year older and had gone off to Spain for their summer holidays. What was I going to do? Watch TV with my parents? Go fishing? In truth, I still liked a spot of fishing now and again. But the people you had to look at on the banks of the local canals, lakes, and gravel pits were generally such greasers or old men, it made me embarrassed to be seen with them. So if I did go fishing, it would be early mornings in the week, when no one was around.

Davy wolfed down his burger, glugged his coffee at lightning speed, and pulled out a fag. The flash bastard had a pack of du Mauriers. I stuffed the rest of my burger down my throat and caught his eye so that he'd offer me one. Bummer did the same. Soon we were filling the blue tin ashtray with lovely, long, turdlike ashes, choking the cafe with thick blue smoke, giving the stark, ugly little joint a bit of atmosphere.

I looked over and noticed one of the Pakis lighting up a Park Drive, and he caught my eye for a second but quickly shifted his gaze back to his coffee. He knew better than to stare at anybody who looked like us. Not that we were violent types, Davy, Bummer, or myself, but a lot of Moddy Boys were, and Pakis were prime targets, always getting done in. I'd seen it happen enough to be familiar with that sick feeling you got when some little bovver boy wrapped his forehead around the bridge of some poor fat Paki's nose and the rest of the pack put the boot in. In town, it usually happened at night, after they threw everyone out of the pubs. But on the coast, at Brighton or Bournemouth, whole armies of bovver boys attired identically would pound the streets like robot clones in broad daylight searching for Pakis, lone greasers, French kids, anyone whose appearance or origin rubbed them the wrong way. One bloke from the pack—usually the smallest—would confront the helpless victim, and with the rest of the gang around him leering like evil itself, the short-arse little Hitler would taunt the victim to tears before grabbing him by the lapels and nutting him. The rest would put the boot in, and then off they'd go, well pumped up and eager for more.

That, as I say, wasn't my style—or Davy's or Bummer's. We were in it for the fashion, the music, the birds. The look was the best. The music was Tamla, ska, and stax— obviously the best—and the birds were the smartest, cutest, and best dressed and had to know how to dance. In 1966 there was nothing smarter to be than a cropped-haired, bovver-jacketed Moddy Boy. Strangely enough, a pinstripe suit was well smart, too! That was, schizophrenically, as Moddy as it comes. I myself had three suits: a pinstripe with patch pockets, a dove-grey number with no tail slit, and an orangey job with a deep tail slit and three flap pockets—a bit sudden, I suppose, but I'd pulled birds in it.

Davy pushed back his chair, which made a rattling squeak on the dirty lino floor, and went up to the counter to get three more coffees. Me and Bummer lit up some Embassys and put combs through our hair. Kevin had acquired the name Bummer in school—from me, of course—because it sounded good coupled with his surname. He seemed sort of resigned to it, even though it had homo connotations.

Davy returned with the white cups and saucers brimming with steaming coffee and we sat around preening, smoking, and chatting. As more dull customers sloped into the Wimpy, we got around to talk of violence and hard nuts. That's when the name "Aub" came up. Davy and I had seen Aub around, heard a few legends about his hardness, but Kevin claimed to have actually met him a few times.

"Really hard is Aub," said Kevin, blinking his pale eyes through the smoke and poking his specs back on his nose, an annoying mannerism that Davy and I used to imitate behind his back. Bummer's cropped hair was reddish and thin, and you knew he'd be bald before he reached thirty.

"You know 'im, don't ya?" I asked, warming up for a story.

"Met him a few times," said Bummer. "He was in here last week."

Davy glanced nervously out at the High Street, now fairly busy with shoppers trudging through the inevitable drizzle. "Was he?" asked Davy, pulling on his fag and sticking his tongue out, the better to savour the tobacco taste.

"Yeah, he came with some other bloke and a bird. They had a Wimpy and coffee."

"Smart," I said.

"Did I tell you what happened last weekend? On Station Road?"

"What? What?" chorused me and Davy.

"Aub was walking across Station Road, y'know, just poodlin' along, head down like, and this red Mini comes up and the bloke in it starts beeping his hooter at Aub, y'know, and Aub is casual—just strolling across the street."

"Yeah?"

"So Aub stops when he sees that this bloke's beeping at him, right?"

"Right."

"And so he sort of sidles out of the Mini's way, and as it passes he swings around and boots it in the door! Fucking great dent in it! And then he just keeps strolling off across the street—like nothing happened!"

"Fuckin' 'ard!" enthused Davy with a whoosh of smoke.

"Hard bastard, eh?" I said, in awe of the legendary Aub.

I reached into my blue bovver jacket, pulled out a pack of Players No. 6, and offered them around. Facing the counter, I could see the thin Italian who ran the Wimpy Bar cranking up the Gagglia machine; the smell of hot milk reached my nostrils. Kevin, who sat opposite me, suddenly made a sort of gulping motion, blinked rapidly, and pushed his wire-framed specs back up his nose, even though they seemed about as far back as they could go. Automatically, me and Davy turned to see whatever had caught Bummer's eye and there, following the rush of air as the door opened, was Aub, trailed by a couple of his mates, all togged out in Moddy Boy uniform.

I felt sweat prickling through my short brown hair and my mouth went dry. I knew the others felt the same. Aub brushed by, inches from Davy's left arm, and gave us a small nod of recognition as he and his mates went straight to the table behind us and pulled out the chairs, making ominous squeals on the lino. I wondered if Aub had some kind of telepathic sense, if somehow he'd felt us talking about him.

"Oi! Free espressos, Dino!" demanded one of Aub's mates, a pinheaded chap with a parka and a crash helmet under his arm.

Dino, the Wimpy Bar Italian, quickly hustled over, balancing three foaming "espressos," even though Wimpy's was strictly counter service.

Davy brushed his hand over his face, threw a little

glance at me, and uttered a small, stifled laugh that said it all. I took a pull from my No. 6, not realizing that I'd been sucking so hard on it since Aub walked in that I was smoking the filter. I nearly gagged on the acrid, foamy flavour. Stubbing it out in the overflowing blue tin ashtray, I wondered what to do. Should I suggest we go down to Maccarri's or would that look funny, leaving as soon as the massive presence of Aub had arrived? On the other hand, if I went up and got more coffee, I'd almost have to brush past Aub, who was sitting at the end of his gang's table. It was one thing hearing stories about Aub and seeing him walking around town, surly as you like, but being in such close proximity, especially after he'd acknowledged our presence, like he'd seen *us* around—well, that was unnerving, to say the least.

So we sat there sort of quiet and Davy pulled out his nice red and white du Maurier box and we lit up, even though I'm sure Davy and Bummer's mouths were as dry as mine. Then Bummer, tactless bastard that he was, said, "Hey, Brian, you getting the third round, mate?" and I felt lumped with the task and too self-conscious to talk about leaving just yet. I knew as the others did that we just had to hang around, for some indefinable reason, in the presence of Aub.

Up I got, fumbling for my wallet as I tried to negotiate the now infinitely long walk past Aub's table to the counter. As I drew level with the pinheaded bloke, he threw a quick glance at me. I didn't look down at him, but with an alarming lack of self-control, found my eyes drawn like magnets toward Aub. A split second before I drew level with him he looked up at me, once again, with some vague sense of camaraderie. He didn't even know my name; he couldn't, I felt, even *really* be sure he'd seen me around before, but I suppose he remembered the briefest of connections with Bummer. Aub made the tiniest upward head motion, and though he was one of those blokes who seem to have no eyes but are all slit, so to speak, I thought I caught a hard twinkle of light—black light—catching the glare of the Wimpy Bar's fluorescent bulbs.

It was all over in a flash and I was at the counter, pulling a ten-bob note from my wallet and oh so casually asking Dino for three espressos, feeling like half a dozen pairs of eyes were burning into the back of my neck. I managed somehow to balance the drinks and return to our table without mishap, edging gingerly past Aub and his mates. In the ashtray, my du Maurier was still burning and I grabbed it quick and took a long pull. I wondered briefly if I'd gone up in my friends' estimation, even though all I'd done was walk past a table with three blokes sitting at it! Still, I hadn't bollixed it up, had I? I hadn't slipped and spilt boiling coffee all over them or copped any hostile looks. I felt pretty good getting that little glance from Aub, who seemed to spend a lot of his time with his small dry lips pursed, his brow knotted, and his slitty little eyes concealed.

The three of us sat there quietly, watching as the Pakistanis in their paint-splattered dungarees got up and left, flicking our eyes occasionally at Aub's party, who were chortling amidst sips of coffee. Then, abruptly, Aub's mates rose to leave, making their chairs scrape loudly, which sent a shiver of apprehension through me. Aub, however, wasn't going anywhere, and as his friends left, he said, "Well, fuck off, then!" in a matey manner. They laughed and headed out the door.

Aub sat at the table fiddling with his spoon, looking straight at us. Bummer turned round for an instant and his eyes must have met Aub's slits. Before I had time to get my saliva working again, Aub had pushed off from his chair and sauntered over to us, plunking his thick-set frame in the spare chair next to Bummer, right opposite Davy.

"Alwight?" he said in his grainy voice, common as muck.

"Hullo, Aub, how's it going?" asked Bummer, his middle-class accent sounding soppy as hell.

"Cunts 'ad to go and pick up Bill's muvver at the station—comin' in from Byfleet she is, cuh!"

"Got to look after mother," said Bummer cheerily. But there was a shake in his voice and he kept pushing those specs up his nose like he was trying to knock his own eyeballs out.

"Wass your name 'en, eh?" Aub asked, his face pointing at Bummer's, but his eyes closed in that very English working-class yobbo fashion.

"Kevin," said Bummer.

"An' oo are these?" he asked, flicking his head toward me and Davy.

"Davy and Brian," answered Bummer.

"Davy and Brian?"

"Yeah," I managed to splutter.

"Alwight," grunted Aub.

"All right," echoed Davy, coolly enough. I did not envy him sitting opposite Aub like that. Aub had parallels on, steel toe–capped Doc Martens, and a faded T-shirt, sort of mauvish colour, with red braces pinching into his big-boned frame. He wasn't a giant—just hard. Impenetrable. At that moment it seemed as if no fist in the world, no forehead, no boot, could ever make the slightest impression on him.

"Thursday, Aub gets engaged," said Aub out of the blue. He said it as if he were talking about a trip to the butcher's or the newsagent's.

"Engaged?" asked Davy.

"Yeah, I don't fuckin' know . . . might as well, I s'pose," chuckled Aub with a little grin. I almost asked "Who to?" but thought better of it.

"Dew get in bovver couple a weeks ago?" he asked suddenly, and although his eyes did not rest upon me, his demeanor had shifted its blocky angles in my direction. I noticed a scar above Aub's left eyebrow. His hair was ginger-coloured, not reddish like Bummer's, but real ginger and brutally cropped, not even enough there for layering in the back.

"Uh . . . yeah," I stammered, not knowing how he could possibly know or be concerned with such a thing. "Yeah, at the Ata, Friday night. How . . . how did you know, Aub?" Christ I was getting familiar now . . . I'd said his name! I wondered briefly what his first name was. Nobody ever mentioned it. Aub, I knew, was short for his surname, which was Aubrey.

"Aub knows, Aub knows," he confided, tapping his strong little nose. "Aub's fiancée knows your bird—the one it was about. Wass 'er name? Anne? That it?"

"Yeah," I answered, astonished, "Anne, right. I was just dancin' with her on that little stage in the corner and this little bloke—"

"I know, I know," interrupted Aub. "The Aub knows the details, mate. Some of my mates saw it 'appen, too. It was the Addlestone boys wot did it."

"Was it? I don't know what 'appened really, I was just—"

"I know," Aub interrupted again. "Pillheads. Fuckin' lot of 'em were on purple 'earts. Fuckin' pillboys wot done you—lucky there was only a few of 'em . . . could a been a fuckin' riot! Dew get 'urt, mate?"

"Nah, nah . . . bloody nose . . . bloody arm or somethin'. Cut me arm somehow. Nothin'," I said, proud of myself.

"Carryin' razors," insisted Aub. "They was probably carryin' razors. Yer lucky you didn't get sliced up. Wot? Dey nut yer, then they all put the boot in? That it?"

"Yeah," I agreed.

"Don't like that 'appenin' to my mates," said Aub. "The Aub might seek revenge."

I felt the blood surging through me like an express train. First Aub's bird knew my bird; second, he knew about the aggro I'd got into and who the perpetrators were; and third, I'm suddenly his mate! I pulled out my fags and offered them around (Aub didn't accept one—he didn't smoke), feeling lightheaded with the sense of in-crowd bonding that had firmly gripped our scratched-up Formica table. Aub was right about the pills. The little bastard who had started it had come right up to my face while I was dancing next to Anne as "The Guns of Navarone" by the Skatalites was pounding through those giant speakers. He'd mumbled incomprehensibly to me, up so close that I could smell his breath. Finally, I just said "Fuck off" to the little creep, and that's when he grabbed the lapels of my pin-stripe and nutted me in the face—which of course sent me down like a nine pin. And then the rest of his mates started kicking the bejesus out of me as I curled into a fetal position. The whole place—the pounding music, the boots, the blackness, and the ultraviolet lights—began spinning around like a car crash. But I'd been dancing for hours and I suppose my adrenaline was so up that I didn't feel a thing. When someone nuts you—if it's done properly, that is—it's all over instantly. It feels like you've run into a wall in the dark. But this idiot hadn't quite hit the bridge of my nose square on, so I only bled for a short while.

I remembered walking outside with Anne and some of her friends and laughing about it. The girls were worried, but I wasn't bothered much. After a spot of fresh air, we went back in and kept right on dancing until the place closed. It had been, apart from the aggro, a great night.

The place was packed to the rafters and hot as hell, and sweat was dripping off the black walls. I loved the Atlanta — the "Ata," as we called it. It was much better than the Agincourt — also known as the "Adge" — in Camberley. Camberley was such a middle-class dump. Woking was better, more working class. But that meant a rumble was more likely.

After we'd gone back into the Ata and resumed dancing — me dabbing my nose with a bloody hanky and this little slice on my wrist — I never got bothered again. The perpetrators just seemed to have vanished. I didn't know why they'd decided on me for their bit of fun that night, but I do remember the thought crossing my mind that it was because I was dancing with Anne.

I'd been in bovver before, naturally, and it was usually because of a girl. Anne was a sexy little thing — fourteen, but she looked much older. I can't remember exactly how we met, but I think it was at the Ata, dancing. Since then I'd been sort of going out with her. We'd gone to the cinema a few times and the last time, in the back row, I'd got my hand down her bra and she'd wanked me off in my trousers. She had lovely tits — really big for her skinny little body and so pert, yet so soft, I'd felt like my fingers would disappear into them forever. I could understand someone being jealous. Anne told me that her parents visited relatives on the weekend sometimes and that they left her in the house by herself — she'd said it like an invitation. I was pretty sure that if I got her alone in her house with a rubber johnny she'd let me shag her. Whenever I thought about this, I'd be walking around with a hard-on for hours. But most weekends Anne's parents weren't going anywhere and she was always knocking about with her friends, so I wondered if it would ever happen.

"Tonight," said Aub, "a little bird tells me — mate of mine I saw last night at the Pearly — that your Addlestone friends might be at the Ata again. Brian, me ole mate, I fink one of 'em really fancies your bird, Anne."

"D'you go to the Pearly last night, Aub?" asked Davy. The Pearly Orchid was a giant dance hall in Pearly that me and him went to once. A great place for pulling birds. We'd got a couple in his motor that night and got gobbled good and proper.

"S'wot I said, ain't it?" said Aub. He scratched his head and threw a few dark looks around the Wimpy Bar, which was becoming crowded with lunchtime shoppers.

"You planning on going to the Ata tonight, boys?"

"Yeah," I confirmed, "big ska night, Saturday."

"Alwight. Alwight," said Aub, and he got up to leave. "My fiancée's goin' wiv your Anne, Brian. And if those Addlestone cunts try anythin', I might just be around for a bit of bovver, know wot I mean? See ya later."

And with that announcement hanging in the greasy, smoky air of the Wimpy, Aub walked out, little lips pursed, slitty eyes on the floor, his barrel chest aimed square for the High Street.

Davy, Bummer, and myself knocked around Woking

for a while that afternoon, not doing anything in particular, letting out the odd whoop of amazed laughter at our sudden, newfound proximity to the great Aubrey. It was hard, basically, to concentrate on anything else. We ran into Steve, a big, slow-witted, one-eyebrowed Moddy Boy from Chobham who always suggested the same thing whenever I saw him: "Les go to the Chinese for a bowl of soup." Which we did. We stared at the flock wallpaper and the little Chinese coolies and Oriental bridges and spiky pine trees in blue that adorned the soup bowls; and we talked about Aub, filling Steve in on the morning's conversation and speculating on what might happen if those Addlestone boys showed up at the Ata.

"Fuckin' great if they do," enthused Steve. "Aub'll fuckin' kill 'em!"

We made a lot of whooshing sounds, well chuffed with ourselves.

After the bowl of soup, I took the 44 bus home, feeling so pepped up I barely noticed the journey. After dinner — which was a nice rabbit stew that my mum had made — I took a bath, then got togged up in my pinstripe, white shirt, red tie, and brogues. I spent half an hour combing my hair and studying myself in the mirror.

By about 7:30 P.M. the drizzle had left off completely, but an autumn chill was in the air. Outside the Ata the crowd was gathering, preening and posturing by the black entrance doors. As the 44 slowed down at the bus stop, I looked at the scene through the bus window and felt the lightning bolts of nerves shoot through my guts.

Just as I disembarked, Bummer came along on his Lambretta Ll 150 and pulled over by the curb.

"Hop on!" he yelled over the revving engine, and I did. There was nothing smarter than to arrive at the front of a dance hall on a scooter wearing a suit. Of course, it would have been even keener if I'd been driving the thing.

As Bummer dropped me off, smack outside the door (causing surreptitious but no less admiring glances from the horde of Moddies posing there), I noticed the back of Aub's head disappearing inside. I could almost feel the blast of the bass end of a Prince Buster tune issuing out of that black cave. I saw someone I vaguely knew—a tall, pasty-faced, skinny bloke who smacked his red braces against his white shirt as he talked to two little fellas in suits—and I stood around with him for a while, smoking and chatting and eyeing up the birds. Then Bummer, who had been parking his scooter, came along and we posed for a while longer, hoping to run into Davy but all the time keeping an eagle eye out for the Addlestone boys.

"Aub's in there," I said to Bummer.

"Did you see Anne yet?" he asked.

"Nah . . . oh, 'ere she is!"

Around the corner, past a throng of blokes hanging about in a tight bunch, came Anne and another girl, all slinky and made up to the nines. They both walked—like all the little Moddy birds—with one arm sort of dangling by their sides, as if it was broken or something; Anne's face was caked with really thick Pan-Cake and her eyebrows were almost nonexistent. I thought she looked dead sexy,

38

what with her perfect tits bouncing under her white frilly-necked blouse and her short black skirt and black shoes.

She came up and kissed me on the lips, causing some blokes to let out a few jeers—which of course made me feel great—and then she introduced her friend Jill, who turned out to be none other than Aub's intended. Jill was altogether a different type. She was demure—Moddy, yes, but hardly the flighty, demonstrative, sexy type like Anne. Jill was a quiet little thing who didn't have a lot to say. But she seemed sweet enough, and in a funny way you could see Aub taking to a girl like that—sort of a fatherly, pro-tective aura about it.

"I saw Aub goin' in," I said to Jill; she just gave a little twitch of her shoulder and a shy smile. Her eyes were brown and quite large, making up for the lack of eyeball on the Aub. She had brown hair in the current style—short and straight with long false sideburns coming down well past her ears. Anne's hairdo was identical, but blond—peroxide, of course.

Anne looked nervous and kept throwing sidelong glances up and down the street every time another knot of Moddy Boys came swaggering along. She seemed espe-cially interested in the scooters racked alongside each other in the car park, all sparkly in the thin evening sunlight with their coloured side panels, chrome crash bars, and jumble of rearview mirrors.

"Let's go in," she announced suddenly, and without a moment's hesitation we paid our two bob, got stamped on the backs of our hands, and plunged into the rectangular, throbbing black room, already half full with jerking shapes under the purple ultraviolets.

Anne grabbed my hand and we threaded our way toward the front to the strains of Jackie Wilson's "Higher and Higher," a thrill going through me as he hit the stratosphere with his crystalline falsetto. By the time we reached the small half-moon-shaped stage in the corner—the stage where I'd been nutted two weeks previous—the DJ was playing "Shake," and me, Bummer, Anne, and Jill began dancing, doing those stiff arm jerks and slidey leg motions that were the current style in the soul clubs. We'd been performing this dance for ages and what was great about it—what was so amazing, really—was that none of the dancers on the crap pop shows on TV were doing anything like it. You'd think that some chinless wonder TV pop show producer would actually go to a real Moddy club, dragging a few TV audience dancers with him, check out the action, and then copy it for *Top of the Pops,* or *Thank Your Lucky Stars,* or whatever bollocks was the current hit. But no, people like us had to watch those spastics and suffer our parents and aunties saying things like: "You do all that stuff, don't you, Brian? You should get on there! Write up. Write up to the TV and get on one of those shows—you can dance, can't you?" You'd feel like you were going to grind your teeth to dust watching those clowns who were five years out of date, and it was just plain disgusting how this crap was supposed to represent what young people were really up to. No wonder there was a lot of violence about. It was enough to make anyone violent.

Davy had appeared by now and slipped into the routine, wearing a plain blue suit and a white shirt with big cuffs floating like ghosts on the end of his sleeves. The Ata was gradually filling up. Before long, the place would become so packed that people would start climbing onto the small stage, which was great, because when you were up there, half the place could see you and you felt like a king. No one got onto the big stage, though — the one where bands like Prince Buster and the All Stars and the Skatalites played — because the management kept it covered with a black velvet curtain. The security didn't really like anyone on the small stage either, but when the place was packed, they often turned a blind eye.

After half an hour of solid dancing to everything from Motown to Stax to Trojan to Len Barry's "One, Two, Three," I got a thirst on and peeled away from our group, which now included the tall, pale, skinny bloke I'd been talking to outside, and a few other couples. The Coke was sold down in the pit where the pinballs were. It was bright as sunshine in there away from the ultraviolets, and full of Moddy Boys playing pinball and hustling around the counter for soft drinks. I got a Coke, lit a fag, and looked around for Aub, but there was no sign of him. He hadn't appeared on the dance floor either, which wasn't surprising, really. Aub wasn't the dancing type.

Halfway through my Coke, I happened to notice a group of blokes in the corner by the Paul Bunyan pinball table. As I spotted them, one, a stocky little fella, caught my eye and glared at me like malice itself. It was the Addlestone boys, and I could tell by those intangible threads of connection zipping across the room that there were more of them than this one group of half a dozen or so. As I was trying to pick out who was who in the smoky crowd, the little bloke — I knew instinctively he was the one who had nutted me — shoved his way across the room, came right up to me with his brutish forehead sweating and his grey eyes bulging like ball bearings, and hissed, "You're dead!" And then he turned and walked back to his mates, who were sneering and chuckling.

I felt like I was split in two. One half of me shuddered and went all clammy and panicky, whilst the other half wanted to kill this little bastard who had the nerve to ruin my good time. But I had a bad sinking feeling that the first half, the clammy, nervous, nauseous one, was going to gain ground. I put my Coke bottle on the counter and made for the dance floor, gulping for saliva that just wasn't there.

Pushing through the dancers, I couldn't help praying I'd bump into Aub, but he didn't seem to be anywhere. All those faces and bodies, jerking and twitching to "Phoenix City," looked like robots gone berserk in slow motion. Finally, I popped out of the tunnel of people, as if I'd just run the gauntlet, and found my little clique. They were dancing on obliviously, right under the lip of the half-moon stage. I caught Anne's eye, and she gave me a tight-lipped look. I started dancing but felt disembodied and grooveless. Then I put my arm around Anne, smelling her liberally dosed, musky perfume and feeling the intense warmth of her firm back.

"Your mate from Addlestone's 'ere again," I bellowed in her ear, trying to cut through the screaming horn section blasting from the giant speakers not five feet away. She looked at me, her face burning with guilt, and I thought she was going to cry.

"What's goin' on?" I implored, and we stopped dancing as I put my arms around her hot, slim body. But she just buried her face against my chest and shook her head as the crowd hit the stop-chorus in unison: "Phoenix City!!!" And then Anne looked up at me, her small dark eyes glistening, and I could see her red lips mouthing the words "I'm sorry." I felt like I was sinking into the floor. I looked over her shoulder at the cuff of my jacket, mesmerized by the fluff sticking up like twigs under the purple ultraviolet light, and I couldn't put a thought together in my head.

An eerie stillness gripped the place; I felt the malevolent presence of the Addlestone boys breathing down my neck. I turned, and there was the short-arse, square-headed little brute who had it in for me, ten feet away, his very presence causing the crowd to part like waves, his mates around and behind him with their Levi's, braces, and bovver boots.

He came at me almost at a run. I instinctively pushed Anne away and she fell screaming into Davy and Jill and the tall, pallid, skinny bloke. But because I'd seen him coming and knew what to expect, the vicious runt had blown the nutting technique, which requires the dual elements of proximity and surprise. His only effective method of attack was the old karate kick, which he performed at lightning speed, hitting me square in the chest. Of course, the least effective way of putting a man down is to hit him in the chest. I just staggered back a few feet and bounced off the lip of the stage with my spine. My forearms moved of their own accord to cover my face as I prepared for the next blows, which I figured would come from about ten places at once as his mates moved in. But he never got the chance to follow his karate kick, and his mates suddenly stopped dead in their tracks. Aub, who must have been lurking in the darkness all the time, appeared out of nowhere and, in a move that took a split second, grabbed matey around the neck with one hand, lifted him clean off the floor, turned him around like a rag doll, and nutted him twice in the face with sickening smacks that you could feel through the music, which happened to be the opening chords to one of the few white acts that we tolerated—the Spencer Davis Group, doing "Gimme Some Loving." Well, the little bastard was annihilated, and Aub just dropped him on the floor like he was a toy. And then all hell broke out.

At some point in the fracas, after I had put the boot into a few Addlestone heads myself, I got hold of Anne and screamed at her for some explanation. Aub's words in the Wimpy Bar that morning rang in my head: "Aub's fiancée knows your bird—the one it was about."

" 'The one it was about,' Anne!" I yelled. She could hear me now as she huddled in the corner, the arms of Jill and another girlfriend around her, because the DJ had stopped the music and people were rushing for the exit.

Anne was sobbing and shaking her head and I could tell that whatever this problem was, it was deep, dark, and secret and she wasn't gonna spill that easily. So I turned away with a disgusted cuss and rejoined the punch-up that was still going on, although with a little less vigour by now. The short-arse Hitler was still on the floor, his face like a squashed tomato, and it looked like the Woking boys had the advantage over the Addlestone crew, who were beginning to peel away, holding their bleeding noses and catching the bloody drips from their mouths so that their clothes wouldn't get too messed up.

Suddenly, someone thought to kill the ultraviolets and put the house lights on. The place lit up cold and harsh, litter and bottles all over the floor like there'd been a Christmas party. Aub saw me and grinned. I walked in his direction; his back was toward the big stage and his red head was framed against the black velvet curtain. There were people milling around, some who had been involved in the fight and others who wanted to say they were there and smell the blood. From behind one group of blokes, this Addlestone boy appeared, wearing a suit, looking fairly unscathed. I didn't even know he was one of them until he shot up to Aub's back quick as grease and hit him in the neck with a sharp, stabbing motion. Aub winced and flailed around, grasping the air behind him pathetically. But it was too late. The bloke was gone, pounding through the litter on the thinning dance floor, almost knocking a straggling couple over as he disappeared through the black front doors.

Aub stood there and looked at his hand, which had been rubbing his neck, almost as if he had just gotten a mosquito bite or an itch. But his hand was covered in blood and I knew he'd been knifed. The police arrived and cleared the place, leading Aub out to the ambulance along with the short-arse bloke who started the trouble; he was just coming to, staggering around like he didn't know what day it was.

In the hospital, Aub lay on a cot with a tube up his nose and a drip in his arm. He'd lost a lot of blood and looked pale, but was quite cheerful. The nurses said we had five minutes and that he needed to rest—it was two A.M. by now and me, Davy, and Bummer were there, along with Jill, Aub's girl.

"They raped 'er, Brian," said Aub. "That little bastard I flattened and one of 'is mates. He was going out with 'er and she wanted to end it, and they was on the common at Byfleet and 'e got mad and raped 'er. Then the other bloke took a turn. Still thinks 'e's got some 'old over 'er—that's 'is problem. Still thinks 'e owns 'er. Jealous as fuck is the little cunt. Tell 'im, Jill. That's wot 'appened, in it?"

Jill looked at me meekly, her mascara running in streaks under her big wet eyes. And then the nurses returned and shoved the lot of us out. Bummer gave me a lift home on the back of his scooter and Davy drove off in his motor, taking Jill with him to drop her at her mother's house on the outskirts of Woking in one of the endless, sprawling new estates.

I saw Anne only once after that, before she and her family moved to Kent, where her dad had landed a plum new civil service job. She was walking down Woking High Street with a bloke who had long hair and a frilly, purple shirt. She left him in a record store and came out to talk to me. She told me she was going out with him because he looked just like Davy Jones from the Monkees.

"Any girl would," she said. "Any girl would."

"But he's cross-eyed!" I pointed out, watching him stare at us suspiciously through the record store window. Anne just shrugged and said she'd better get back to him. I considered making a smart comment as she turned her back and clicked off in black heels, miniskirt riding her bum, but I said nothing, and turned off up the road to the Wimpy Bar.

As for Aub, I'd see him about occasionally, knocking around town or in the Ata. Sometimes he'd rub his neck, twist his head to give you a good view, and say, "Look at that, will ya! Beauty, ain't it?!" meaning the one-inch purple scar where the blade had gone four inches into his thick shoulder. Funnily enough, our shared experience didn't mean that me and him were to become firm friends, and we remained two blokes with two separate lives who nodded to each other now and again. To him, the whole affair was just another violent incident in a life studded with violent incidents, and he wasn't going to invite me home for tea with his mother because of it.

Sometimes, on those empty Saturdays in Woking, Davy, Bummer, and myself would find our table graced by the Aub's presence. Over Wimpy Burgers and sweet, foamy espresso, we'd have a laugh about the Addlestone boys and how the little pillhead that Aub had flattened was now doing a stretch in Wormwood Scrubs for Grievous Bodily Harm, and how the bastard deserved to be there. I didn't mind in the least that Aub had fought one of my battles for me, because he didn't mind either. As for Anne . . . I don't remember anyone ever mentioning her again.

## chloroform

'**ve** gotta get these boys in!" said Andy, banging another metal frame across the concrete floor toward the autoclave. "Look, it's nearly five o'clock and I get these boys from Frank and he wants them done. Get these boys in!"

Mick and I watched Andy, blathering on with his head down, ripping the cages out of the frames and clanging them into the machine, the tang of hot water and steam filling the air in the washroom. Andy lurched up to us and pulled his old gloves off, sensing an unlikely audience. Even though our interest in his rage was purely selfish, he was too dimwitted to pick up on it and made the best of our concerned looks, head shakes, and chin scratchings.

"Frank just gave you those to do, Andy? What, at this time of day?" I asked.

"This time!" he squeaked. "Nearly bastard five o'clock bloody fat pig Frank! I'll never get on my bike by five now bloody bastard Frank!"

"No, I doubt if you'll make five, Andy," I said, pursing my lips and staring at my watch. Andy turned back to the autoclave. Mick and I nudged each other and put our hands up to our mouths to conceal our mirth.

The Animal Virus Research Institute, Purfleet, Surrey, boasted some motley characters for employees, but none as thick and outlandish as Andy. When he first got the job of General Dogsbody six months ago, we could barely believe it. Workers peeked out of the small windows in the blocks to check out this little bloke with the splay-footed walk and flat head as Frank gave him his tour of duty. Decked out in a fresh brown lab coat, Andy was obviously mentally defective, and we wondered if this was some new government scheme, what with that half-wit girl student who'd spent a week with us recently—the one who'd memorized the weather broadcasts for shipping from Radio 4: "Dogger bank, thirty-five latitude fifteen longitude, nor'easter half mile from Jenkins Sandbank. Dogger bank, Dogger bank." That's all she said, like a broken record.

A lot of the young guys like myself had become cynical about working for the institute. It was a filthy job with no future, full of bitter, middle-aged people constantly reminding any males under the age of twenty-two that they were not really men yet. Conversation lasting longer than a few minutes would inevitably lead to the subject of age and how us "boys" would soon reach our peak — mentally, physically, and sexually; that it was all downhill from now on. Us "boys" were supposed to be thinking about marriage and houses and mortgages and pensions and the rest of the crap that had turned these people into old codgers while they were still teenagers.

And now this Andy, phutting into the car park on his Honda 50 every morning, twitching between the blocks with his uncombed flat black hair and his feckless grin; he made you want to clout him. He was like a mosquito, buzzing around the place in small, unnecessary bursts of static energy, like he had a battery inside him that switched on at random and fired him between the rectangular build-ings of the animal husbandry area like a pinball.

"Well, Andy, we'll leave you to it, then, right, Mick?" I said.

"Right, Brian, better get going. Look at that, it's a min-ute to five already, see ya, Andy," said Mick.

"I'll get these boys in! I'll get 'em in yet!"

Andy smashed a cage frame into the dirty white con-crete wall and grabbed his hose and started spraying it while the autoclave droned like a great animal, sterilizing the mouse cages.

Mick and I left him mumbling and smashing, and went up to F Block and clocked out just as it hit five. We joined Marge and Mal in the tiny room where we took our breaks and ate our sandwiches, next door to Frank's office.

"You should see Andy down in the washroom," I said to them.

"Why? What's goin' on?" asked Marge hungrily, her black eyes darting past me, on the alert for Frank.

"Frank's given him all this stuff to do and he's goin' berserk," I said under my breath, knowing that Frank was within earshot, leaning over his books like a great toad.

"Oo, blimey, mate!" said Marge, and she gave Mal a little nudge. Mal let out a quiet snort of amusement. We heard the chair shift next door and Frank emerged, waddling up to the entrance to our room.

"See you all tomorrow, then," he said, leaning his head in.

"G'night, Frank," we chorused as he walked off in his dark blue pinstripe. Frank hailed from the North Country and was an extremely short man, almost as wide as he was high. He exuded that typical Northern bossiness and a superior, officious manner that you couldn't help but find unpleasant. There were wrong ways to do things and Frank's way—that's all there was to it in his book.

" 'Ere," said Marge, looking to make sure he'd gone, "I saw him bendin' over today, pickin' somethin' up, and his balls were hangin' down like a great bulldog's!"

"Ooer!" exclaimed Mal.

"You should see Andy," I said, grabbing my bomber jacket from its peg, holding it delicately so as not to rub in the odour of mouse shit that seemed impossible to remove completely, however much scrubbing you did.

"Is he hopping mad?" asked Marge eagerly.

"Going bonkers," said Mick.

"Oo!" said the women in unison.

"What are you *boys* doing over the weekend, then, eh?" asked Marge.

"It's Thursday, Marge," said Mal.

"Oh blimey, so it is!" exclaimed Marge. Mick and I said good night and left, smarting at her use of the word "boys." At the age of nineteen you do not want to be called a boy.

Mick and I walked out toward the car park; a cacophony of revving greeted us as everyone got their cars, scooters, and motorbikes going. It was a relief getting out of that place, away from the reek of mice turds; from healthy mice, diseased mice; escaping the endless chittering and the nagging scraping of their tiny feet against the wire-bottomed cages; leaving behind the mops and buckets that we used to clean the red-tiled floors of the cells where the animals were housed; getting away from the clouds of straw dust that clogged up the sinuses and stung our eyes; escaping the flies, the Brasso, and the stinking rags that polished the taps.

It was good to get away from the people, too: Marge and Mal with their clucking and cooing; Terry, the ball-sure Little Hitler with his heavily birthmarked face, his guinea pigs, and his bullshit; Hans, the Kraut with the big nose who was always trying to convert us "boys" to religion; Frank Doyland, the fat boss with his "I'm always right" attitude; Taff, another Northerner my age and a right little chest-out cock o' the walk who worked in D Block with

Terry and boasted continually of how he was fucking the pig-faced girl from A Block, as if she were some prize.

And then there was Andy, who could be infuriating because of his abject stupidity, but truthfully, I preferred him to a lot of the workers because he seemed entirely without malice — as if that part of his brain had been wiped along with all the other parts missing since conception. And anyway, he was about to enter a little business transaction with me: he was going to buy my Lambretta SX150 motor scooter for eighty pounds.

On Friday morning I got straight to work cleaning out the litter trays, scraping the encrusted mouse shit into a rolling rubbish bin and checking the diet scoops, keeping an eye out for tyzers, a disease that periodically swept through the stock like wildfire. When tyzers broke out, we animal technicians were forced to perform purging culls in order to stem its rapid progress.

Neither tyzers nor any other foul degenerative diseases appeared to be raging as I made the rounds, although I had to wring the necks of a few weaklings that looked like likely candidates. Then Marge told me to go into the breeding room and sex a few hundred three-day-olds.

I picked through the pink maggoty babies looking for minute penises, then dropped the males into a big glass jar with cotton wool at the bottom. When I had sorted out the sexes, I took the jar full of wiggling, blind male babies to the storeroom, where I opened a container of chloroform. I soaked a wad of cotton with the chloroform and screwed it into the bottom of the jar, taking care not to inhale too much of the stuff. It was supposed to be addictive; some bloke had got himself fired a year ago after they caught him spread out on the storeroom floor, half unconscious from a sniffing session.

The chloroform soaked into the cotton that the babies were lying on; after I had jammed the top on tight, they soon stopped their wiggling. It was the females that the lab boys needed. Apparently, they ground them up and centrifuged the mush, which was then used in a scientific procedure that enabled research into a cure for foot-and-mouth disease. No one had explained to me why only the females were useful: we were just animal technicians—it was our job to breed them. The people with A levels and college degrees did the research; they worked "inside," as the laboratory facility was called, a place we could never enter. You had to be of a different stamp to go "inside." The insiders were a clean-skinned lot—middle-class people with Rovers and big Wolseleys and curly blond hair. The only time we had contact was in the car park or in the canteen where they took their meals on the other side of the kitchen that bisected the dining room.

After I'd sorted the babies it was tea break; Marge, Mal, Mick, and myself sat in F Block's lunchroom, having tea and snacks, our knees almost touching in the cramped space. Flies buzzed around the bare electric bulb and Mick and I had sport with them, firing rubber bands expertly off our fingers, leaving their small, bloody corpses stuck all over the dirty walls like squashed sultanas. Outside, dark clouds were blustering, bringing intermittent autumn rain.

"Is it today Andy's taking his test?" asked Mal.

"Yeah, today, that's right," I said, getting mildly enthusiastic. Andy still had L plates on his Honda 50 and had taken the morning off to take his driving test in Aldershot. We chuckled at the thought of it. We just couldn't see him passing. I had recently taken my driving test and passed — not for a bike, I'd passed for that years ago, but for a car. That was why I was selling my scooter: I was soon to buy a secondhand Triumph Herald, my first car.

"When's he back? After lunch?" asked Marge.

"Yeah," I answered, "should be a laugh. What 'ave I got to do this afternoon?"

"Room Three still needs mucking out and there's the taps and the floors," said Mick. "I can cover for you."

"Thanks, mate, I'm dying to find out how he did. I'll sneak down there and get a report. I'll push a frame down or something — that'll give me an excuse."

Everyone agreed that I should be the one to get the story from Andy, seeing as he was buying a scooter from me, and besides, I always had people cracking up when I reinterpreted his wild stories. It was the way I told them, I supposed — plenty of dramatic flair.

After lunch, when everyone had settled down and the paths that wound between the blocks were empty, I quietly pushed a cage frame out the door, cocking an eye at Frank, who was in his little room, his back toward me, hunched over his accounting. I pushed the frame through the swing doors and went down to the washroom.

There stood Andy, twitching and cursing, spraying a guinea pig frame with hot water, his lab coat utterly soaked and his ill-fitting grey trousers sticking out over the top of his black gum boots.

"Andy! Hey, mate, how ya doin'? How was the test?"

He turned and looked at me, his one good eye betraying a hint of rage and disappointment. He switched off the hose and, with a grimace, dashed over to the autoclave and jammed open the wheel. Huge billows of steam came out as he reached in and pulled at the boiling hot cages with his tattered gloves. The cages clattered onto the concrete. Andy began stacking them into the frame, cursing as the thing rolled awkwardly in the concave depression of the drainage corner. I approached him carefully, dragging my frame behind me. I didn't want to draw too much attention to it for fear of triggering an even worse reaction from Andy. Sometimes he would get so frustrated at things, he could barely talk.

"What's up, Andy? Give you a hard time, did they?"

He stopped banging the cages and turned around, blinking and twitching.

"I don't know, I did what he said. I did what the snot bastard little bum said!"

"What, Andy?" I asked, trying not to sound too gleeful.

"Well, the man said: You go up Pinder Road and around the block to the main street . . ."

"Yeah."

". . . and then you take the left fork to Squadron Road, past those old barracks . . ."

"Yeah, yeah."

". . . and then you come back past the King's Head on the main street and back onto Pinder Road . . ."

"Right."

". . . and by the time you've done that, he said, you would have done a figure eight."

I visualized the route the test official had given Andy. It was similar to the one they'd given me a few years back when I passed my two-wheeled vehicle test.

"And? And? Did you fail?" I demanded, sensing a real treat in the offing.

"Well, I don't bastard know. I did what the snot bastard said and the fucking little fuck bastard failed me. I got on my bike and got on the road and did a figure eight and he failed me and walked off!"

I could barely contain myself.

"You mean, Andy, you did a figure eight right there on Pinder Road, right in front of the test man?"

"That's it, that's what the snot bastard fucker said. I did a figure eight like he said, a good figure eight, I know what a bastard figure eight is!"

"But Andy, he meant *after* you've driven around all the roads he told you to drive on, you would have *completed* a figure eight. He didn't mean you do a *little* figure eight in front of him. He was just describing the *shape* of the route you had to take."

Andy scratched his greasy, flat black hair and looked up at me with his roving eye, which only occasionally alighted upon the person he was addressing.

"But . . . I did a bastard figure eight!" he exclaimed.

Typical of my conversations with the addled runt, my amusement now evolved into annoyance. There was just no getting through to him; it was like he had a head full of soup. Tiring of hearing about the botched driving test, I turned my attention to the fine points of selling Andy my SX150.

"Andy, you still up for buying my scooter, then?"

"Yeah, I want it, on Monday I'm ready to buy. So I give you twenty pounds . . ."

"Right, you give me twenty pounds down, then ten a month till you've paid the full eighty, all right?"

"All right," said Andy, the dim cogs turning behind his errant, hooded eye. "I give you twenty."

"That's it, Andy. You give me twenty quid, then ten a month till you've paid the full eighty."

"Eighty?"

"Yes, Andy, remember?" I said, fed up with repeating daily this simple hire-purchase agreement that a child could understand.

"So . . . I give you twenty . . ."

"Exactly. The scooter's worth eighty, but you just give me twenty down at first, right?"

"Twenty."

"Right, twenty. Then ten a month till you've paid up,

okay? Look, I'll see you Monday with the money and you can take the scooter. You just have to stick your L plates on, seeing as you didn't pass your test, all right?"

"So . . . I give you twenty . . ."

"Yeah, Andy, twenty. I gotta go."

I left Andy blinking and twitching in the steam and went back to F Block to reenact the driving test fiasco to the others, which left them creased up for the rest of the day.

On Saturday I bought my first car, a secondhand, ice-blue Triumph Herald, for 160 quid, with a little financial help from my old man. It felt great tooling around the suburbs in that car. On Saturday night my mate Dave and I went out drinking; we picked up a couple of birds who were hitching down the A30. They were pretty rough-looking, so we stopped in at the Jolly Farmer, bought them a drink, and then moved off to another pub. Still, it was great being able to do that; to have those four seats and a roof, all cozy like a little house on wheels.

Monday morning, I arrived at work to find a tyzers outbreak in F Block. I had to cull a lot of foul, diseased mice. I had rode in to work on my Lambretta and couldn't wait to get the first installment from Andy and get rid of the thing. Though the scooter was a great machine, I was dying for Tuesday when I could turn up at work in my very own car.

"Hi, Andy," I said, entering the washroom at break. He was sitting in a chair facing the wall, eating a sandwich and drinking tea.

"Ready to become the proud owner of a Lambretta SX150, then, mate?"

Andy pulled his gaze away from a very interesting sheen of condensation on the wall.

"Brian, I've got the money for the scooter, I've got it, twenty pounds. Here it is in me pocket here!"

"Great, Andy, here's the keys, I'm leaving the flyscreen on for you, okay?"

Andy stood up and placed his half-eaten sandwich on the grubby metal seat and shuffled over to me, digging the twenty out of his lab coat pocket. I gave him the keys and a receipt that I'd made up previously. Just then, Terry, the Little Hitler, and Taff, the young Northern cock o' walk, strutted in.

"Eh, fuckin' 'ell, what's this? Money changing hands?" said Taff.

"Give 'im a blow job, Brian?" added Terry sarcastically.

"He's buying my scooter," I answered.

"Shut up, you two bastard bum bastards, you don't get on at me again, my guardian said I should report you to Frank an' I will!"

"Oh fuck off, you little turd," said Taff. "Eh, what's this we hear about your test, then, Andy?" he continued gleefully. "Did some figure eights like a fuckin' ballerina in Aldershot High Street, did we, eh, Andy? Ha ha ha!"

"Gr . . . gr . . . shut up!" bellowed Andy, clenching his tiny teeth and blushing like he was about to burst a blood vessel.

"Silly little twat," spat Taff, and we left Andy steaming like an autoclave.

A month went by during which I proudly drove to work in my Triumph Herald and Andy, resplendent in oversized helmet and goggles (which made him look like a Biggles impersonator), proudly drove to work on his Lambretta SX150 motor scooter. On a drizzly Monday morning at tea break, I strolled down to the washroom to collect my second installment of ten pounds.

I found Andy hunched over in his chair. He was staring at the wall, holding a Spam sandwich in one hand and a colourless flask of tea in the other.

"Hi there, Andy, all right, mate? Going well on the scooter?"

"Eh? Oh hullo, Brian. Yeah, great scooter, goin' well, mate."

"So, it's a month now . . . you, ah . . . you got the ten you owe me, then?"

"Ten?"

"Yeah, the ten."

"What ten?"

"Andy," I said, already wound up. "You gave me twenty down, right?"

"I gave you twenty."

"Right, and now it's a month later, correct?"

"A month."

"So now you give me ten quid, right? And in another month you give me another ten quid, right? And so on until you've paid for the scooter, okay?"

I measured each word slowly and clearly, but judging by the baffled expression on Andy's face, he had either forgotten our agreement or not fully understood it in the first place.

"What?" he asked, genuinely confused.

"YOU OWE ME TEN POUNDS! TEN POUNDS NOW AND TEN EACH MONTH UNTIL YOU'VE PAID THE FULL EIGHTY, REMEMBER?!!"

I bellowed so loudly that my throat hurt, but Andy just sat there blinking in the silent washroom.

"I . . . gave you twenty for the scooter."

"I fucking know you gave me twenty, you twat, but now you still owe me sixty quid, don't you fucking understand, you idiot?"

"But you said it was twenty," said Andy, nervously getting to his feet.

That was it. I lunged forward and grabbed him by the throat, causing his tea, sandwich, and chair to clatter across the concrete floor. As I tightened my grip, his face went red and he flailed at me with his arms. Surprisingly, perhaps due to the manual work he performed daily, he was quite strong. But I was so incensed that I soon had him pinned against the wall and, together with a choke hold, delivered a few punishing knees to the groin. Andy's face creased into a pained, frightened grimace.

"Oi! What's goin' on in here? Stop that at once!"

It was Frank, executing a fast waddle across the wet concrete and grabbing me by the scruff of the neck. I immediately loosened my grip and Andy slumped to the floor, his face changing from bright red to a sickly white.

"What's up here?" demanded Frank as he pushed his fat hand into my chest. I had a real urge to smack him in the mouth but controlled it. Then Hans the Kraut came in and lifted Andy up, checking for damage.

Back at F Block, after I'd explained the hire-purchase fiasco to Frank, he gave me the phone number of Andy's guardian. That evening, I walked to the phone box on the corner and tried to get hold of him. No answer.

The next morning when I arrived at work, I noticed Andy and some scuzzy-looking individual standing by the bike shelter, watching me as I parked. I got out of the car and strolled across the gravel toward them.

"You shouldn't have done that to Andy, you know," said the man in a middle-class accent. "Andy doesn't understand." He had thinning brown hair, ugly horn-rims, and a pinstripe suit so old and faded the pinstripes were barely visible.

"He owes me sixty quid, mate," I said, already balling up my fist.

Andy's guardian reacted quickly and stepped back, pulling Andy with him.

"I'll get the police on you," he threatened, hustling his charge away.

The scruffy pair lurched off down the narrow concrete path that cut across the neat flat lawn and disappeared between the breeding facilities. I stood motionless on the crunchy gravel as other employees walked by me, some with quizzical glances. When I arrived at F Block, Andy's guardian had already said his piece to Frank and was strutting out of the place like he'd just delivered an important proclamation to the Prime Minister. Frank, with his brown tie askew and his fat gut stuck out in the direction of my bony chest, wasted no time in putting me to rights. He pretty much told me to lay off and stomach the loss, like it was my fault or something; I never should have involved the half-wit in a complicated transaction like that in the first place, he said.

I just stood there and bottled it up; I couldn't believe this was happening to me. I hadn't even finished paying off the installments on the scooter myself. Now I was not only stuck with debts on the bike, but also paying for a complete cretin to ride around on it!

Mick attempted to discuss the situation with me, but I was too choked up to be articulate; I just mumbled about getting the money somehow. Marge and Mal thought it all very entertaining and went around clucking and giggling, which made me mad as hell.

At some point in the afternoon, I found myself alone in one of the back rooms polishing a big brass tap that came out of the wall. I felt unconnected to the task I was performing; my hands seemed to belong to someone else. Abruptly, as if an invisible force had taken hold of me, I dropped the rag and walked down to the storeroom at the front of the block. Marge and Mal were cleaning up in one of the rooms and Frank was out making the rounds; I couldn't see Mick anywhere, so I slipped into the storeroom and closed the door behind me.

Sunlight filtered through the little bottle-glass window,

and it was quiet and peaceful as I picked up the chloroform jar and doused a ball of fluffy cotton wool. At first I thought I'd walk down to the washroom, grab Andy around the neck, and stuff the cotton wool into his face until he passed out. But for some reason I dropped it into the "killing jar" and took a little sniff.

I sat down on the red, rubberized tiles and leaned against a metal rack, instantly going dizzy. When the effect wore off, I poured more chloroform into the jar, saturating the cotton on the bottom. I poked my nose into the jar's opening and took another sniff—a deep one this time— and immediately slumped back, banging my head against the rack and letting the jar slide out of my limp hand onto the floor. I felt a tremendous surge, like blood pounding through my head, and then I closed my eyes and drifted off.

The next thing I knew, Frank was shaking me and cursing. I looked up to see his hand slapping my face. His head, which seemed miles away, was floating up near the ceiling; the black hair perched on top of it bounced like flat, burnt straw. Frank was shouting for Marge, and after what felt like hours, I heard echoing footsteps and doors banging. After a moment of silence, someone threw cold water in my face.

I felt all bloated and weird, wondering if I'd been in a car accident. Then I heard Frank yelling, "You idiot, you're fired! That's it, get your cards and get out of here!"

As my senses began drifting back, I staggered to my feet and rolled out of the storeroom with my head still pounding. Mick hovered around me, holding me up every time I drifted into the wall. I lurched outside, gathering an audience as my co-workers came out of the blocks and stared at me in mute fascination. Marge ran out of F Block, holding my jacket. I took it and headed off to the car park, still pie-eyed.

I dozed in my car for a while. It was five o'clock and people had begun to converge in the car park. I started the car and drove off, turning left toward Aldershot instead of right to Purfleet, the direction I normally took home.

I didn't have much of a plan; a numbness had overtaken me, as if I had pushed all my anger and frustration into a deep well. I drove robotically along the country road, between the pines and birches, horse chestnuts and oaks, until I pulled over to the side of the road without a second thought. Within ten minutes, the familiar red and white of my Lambretta SX150 flashed by, and I turned the key in the ignition and eased out after it.

As he negotiated a curve in the road and came to an open grassland area, Andy twisted his head around and looked into the fields gormlessly, the autumn sun glinting off his ridiculous goggles. I was incensed by this image. Hissing like a snake, I jammed my foot down on the throttle.

I must have been doing about fifty when I came up alongside him. In that split second, when his dim wits realized what was going on and the recognition spread across his goggled face, I jerked my steering wheel to the left and hit the front wheel of the Lambretta, causing it to buckle instantly. Like a whirling toy, Andy went flying off into the ditch at the side of the road. The scooter span feverishly on the tarmac and I slowed down and stopped, staring in the rearview mirror as bits of chrome flew like tinsel and the flyscreen cracked off the handlebars like a plastic egg.

Andy popped up in the ditch, his goggles still in place; swaddled in his dirty black leather jacket, he looked like a toad emerging from the earth. As he tried to claw his way to level ground, it appeared that he might have sustained some kind of leg injury. After a couple of attempts to pull himself to safety, he gave up altogether and disappeared into the mud.

I watched the scooter come to a standstill and noticed with satisfaction that both side panels were crumpled and its frame was twisted in a hopeless way. Then I stepped on the throttle and drove to a crossroads where I hooked a right back toward Purfleet. From there I drove home and waited for the police to arrive.

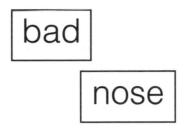

# bad nose

I shut the press down and peeled off my oily overalls, drap-
ing them over the sticky stool where I sat all day at work.
Ronnie the foreman walked by, inspecting the line of fine-
blanking presses, making sure they were switched off and
generally poking around the boxes of product. He'd been
working at the factory for about three months and had
come in like an uppity new broom, tearing around with
annoying, youthful enthusiasm in order to step up production. Stan Lawless, the manager, had hired Ronnie, an am-
bitious little bastard from Basingstoke, to set a fire under
us.

"How's the cold, Brian?" Ronnie asked me as I made

my way to the time clock. "Not gonna keep you away from work tomorrow, is it?"

"Doubt it," I said. "Had it so bloody long I'm gettin' used to it . . . seems like a permanent bloody fixture."

Ronnie swept back his dead-straight, Brylcreemed hair and dashed off to dock the forklift. A hissing sound filled the air, echoing in the high metal rafters of the building as workers shut down their machines. The factory was just one great tin shed with a makeshift walkway halfway up along two walls that led to the offices, giving the place a feeling of impermanence, like it could be torn down any day. It was like working in an oily, clanking gymnasium. I'd been employed for six months and felt fairly settled in, then this hot rod Ronnie comes along and starts muscling around, telling me to take a metallurgy course and pushing the older geezers into working harder and running off more parts per day and all the rest of it. He got up everyone's nose, really.

I shouldn't have been working there at all by rights; a musician is what I should have been. But I'd hardly picked up my old bass guitar in months, and when I did, it was difficult to play because of the cuts on my fingers from handling the huge, sharp sheets of metal that you fed into the presses. Wearing gloves slowed me down, so I never bothered.

The press I had recently been assigned to housed a part that made metal discs for Rank/Wharfdale speakers and took fifteen-foot metal planks that I had to thread in by hand. I was twenty-two and married; making parts for speakers was probably the closest I'd ever get to the music business.

The clock hit five and I punched out and headed off in the drizzle to my old olive-green Morris Minor. Getting in the line of cars that left the small industrial estate every evening at the same time, I drove toward my home three miles away. Once past the glut of traffic at the Cronwell roundabout, I peeled off down Talbot Road through the new estates of pale bungalows squatting in the drizzle and into the narrow, older streets at the back end of Kernley with its sodden village green still littered with the debris of a bonfire left over from Guy Fawkes night. My nose was streaming and my head felt like it was stuffed with cotton wool. I'd had this stinking cold for weeks, months even. I just couldn't shake it. My sinuses had always been terrible, and once, when I was a kid, my mum took me to the doctor to see if I could get them scraped out. The doctor didn't seem too interested in doing anything, so I've just lived with it.

"Christ, you look rough, Brian," said old Len in the village paper shop where I stopped to buy cigarettes. "Still got that cold, then?"

"Yeah, can't get rid of the bastard."

"Well, it's the weather, ain't it? Rain tomorrow, according to the forecast."

"Don't stop, does it?" I said, pocketing the ten Players No. 6, a box of matches, and, as an afterthought, a box of Terry's All Gold for the wife.

I drove up the village main street to Acacia Road,

where our semi-detached house stood in a row of similarly anonymous-looking homes. A year ago, we'd taken out a mortgage on our house, but it was just as damp and cramped as the flat we'd lived in on Market Street in town.

"Dinner's in the oven," announced Sharon as I entered the kitchen at the back of the house. "Still raining?"

"Yeah," I said, pulling off my mac. I fished my hankie out and blew my nose as another chill ran through me.

"Christ, Brian," grumbled Sharon, "why don't you go an' see a bloody doctor! For Christ's sake, it's drivin' me barmy, that cold."

"All right, all right," I said, rumpling the soaked handkerchief and throwing it in the laundry basket, where it sat with some underwear and other used hankies. "Are there any clean ones about?" I asked.

"Is that all I'm good for?" asked Sharon, pulling a TV dinner out of the oven. "Is that it? Cooking, cleaning, washing your disgusting hankies? Is that it?"

"Oh, come on, Sharon," I groaned. "Eh, look. Here's some Terry's All Gold."

I handed her the chocolates, but she gave me a look and dumped the dinner onto the small white plastic table and huffed out to the living room. I heard the TV, some soap opera it sounded like. Sharon tutted and sucked in her breath as she flopped into the threadbare armchair to watch the show.

"Where's the clean hankies?" I shouted from the kitchen.

"Where d'you think they are?" she yelled back, exasperated.

I ate the braised beef and read the sports pages, holding a paper towel under my nose most of the time. Every time I sneezed I could hear Sharon shifting uncomfortably in the other room. She'd had enough of my nose. The continual snuffling was bad enough, but I think the snoring was driving her nuts. According to her, it had gotten so bad she was only getting a few hours of sleep a night.

Have a nap in the day, I told her. But she'd been working mornings at the Kernley post office and said she didn't have time. She had to clean the house in the afternoons, she said, and get me ready for work first thing in the morning. I was helpless, she reckoned, and would never change my clothes or be able to make a sandwich for my lunch without her.

I finished the meal and lit a cigarette, running over the TV page in the paper without much interest. I put the electric kettle on and made some tea.

"Do you want a cup, Sharon?" I shouted through another bout of sneezing.

"No," she answered, changing the TV channel to a game show.

I went into the living room with my tea and pushed the cat off the sofa and flopped down. The sofa was sagging and thick with cat hairs, but it had to do, what with the price of furniture. There was no way we were going to lash out on a luxury like a new sofa. Not with the mortgage and the bills and the repairs I'd had done on the car recently. Not until we'd gotten over this hump, anyway.

"Any Lemsip?" I asked, lighting another cigarette. Sharon took a breath and reached for her packet of Consulates. She'd always smoked menthols, even before I first met her in the pub four years ago. She'd always have a pack of menthols in her bag.

"You know where to find it," she said flatly, lighting up.

Sharon wore a pink bathrobe over her jumper and jeans and her brown hair hung around her face. She was looking a bit plumpish lately, but I couldn't talk, what with the beer gut I'd been cultivating in recent years. I was a good stone overweight myself.

We sat sullenly watching the TV until I felt peckish. There was homemade apple pie in the fridge, so I drifted out to the kitchen to get a piece. I grabbed the pie together with an opened can of Libby's milk and put it on the table. Outside, the rain was coming down in sheets, pounding the guttering and the shed roof.

I got a plate from the cabinet by the oven and sat down at the table, ready to cut myself a slice of pie. For some reason, I sniffed it; it was half gone and I wasn't sure how long it had been in the fridge. Sharon entered the kitchen and saw my nose, hovering over the pie. A big sneeze came over me and I had to quickly turn my head away from the plate and put my hand to my mouth.

"What are you sniffing that for?" she asked.

"I dunno," I said.

"You can't even smell anything with that nose. What are you sniffing it for?"

"I dunno!" I said, getting annoyed. "Just wondered how old it was, that's all."

"It was made yesterday!" She scowled. "You're always sniffing my cooking like there's something wrong with it, and you can't even smell anything anyway. That's what gets me."

I looked at the pie, then cut a piece off and poured the Libby's over it.

"You've been tucking into it, haven't you?" I said.

"So?" she snapped. "I made the bloody thing! Why are you always sniffing about? What's the point?"

"I don't know, Sharon," I said. "I'm not *always* sniffing about. Just this pie, that's all."

"Yes you are," she said. "You had a good sniff at that roast beef I made last Sunday, like it was off or something."

"I think it *was* off," I said.

"No it wasn't, Brian! And what about the sandwich this morning?"

"What about it?" I asked.

"I saw you sniffing it like there was something bad in it."

"I thought it might be leftover roast beef, that's all."

"Oh yeah," she snorted. "I'm going to give you roast beef that's been sitting around all week. As if I would!"

"What was in that sandwich anyway, Spam?"

"Spam?" she exclaimed, helping herself to a piece of pie. "Spam? It was that luncheon meat from the supermarket that you like. Why do you have to go sniffing at it?"

"Dunno," I said, feeling suddenly defeated by the whole conversation.

I sat around eating the pie and blowing my nose until Sharon complained about me using all the Kleenexes, so I went upstairs and pulled two clean handkerchiefs out of the drawer. The roses on the wallpaper depressed me as I sat down on the bed, clicking my ears in order to hear through the stuffiness. My old bass guitar was propped up in the corner by the tallboy. I had a little Rockman gadget and some earphones lying next to it and considered for a moment picking it up and having a go, but then I looked at the cuts on my fingers and decided against it.

"I'm going down the pub," I mumbled when I got downstairs.

"Um," said Sharon distractedly, her attention now fixed on the television.


"You *still* got that cold, Brian?" asked Dosser as I entered the public bar of the White Lion in Cronwell, announcing my presence with a violent sneeze.

"Can't shake the bastard," I said.

Some old Gary Glitter hit was on the jukebox and a group of kids, eighteen- or nineteen-year-olds, were sitting around the tables, drinking lager and lime. A couple of old guys and their wives were throwing darts at the end of the bar. Two of my mates, Dibby and Fred Box, were having a game of shove ha'penny in the alcove. I ordered a pint of bitter.

" 'Ere," said Dosser quietly, lighting up a Rothmans. "I fancy that bird with the tits, don't you?"

I looked at the group of younger people and saw this plump girl in a tight green pullover fiddling with her earrings.

"Got a pair on 'er, ain't she?" I said.

"Christ!" said Dosser, laughing. "Like two little boys under a blanket!"

"Oi, Kev," I called to another mate who sat further down the bar.

"What?"

" 'Ow's business, all right?"

"Yeah, not bad, Brian, not bad. 'Ow's the fine wankin' factory, then, all right?"

"New foreman's a right bloody tosser," I said. "Bloke's a complete nutter. Worse thing is, 'e thinks I should take a metallurgy course or something, y'know? Thinks I wanna better meself or something like that. I dunno, drives me round the bend, 'e does: increase production this, increase production that—nonstop rabbit fuckin' rabbit, know what I mean?"

"Sounds like 'e wants a kick in the goolies, that bloke," said Kev.

"What is it you do anyway, Brian?" demanded George the barman, cleaning a pint glass in a plastic bowl of sudsy water. "I mean . . . what, y'know . . . what are these presses, then?"

I'd explained to George what I did for a living at least twice before, but he was one of those blokes who ask you something, then don't pay attention when you give them an answer.

"They make parts for machines," I explained wearily. "They're like . . . I dunno, presses, you know? You put metal sheets in 'em and punch buttons and they stamp parts out of the metal sheets."

"They can automate that, can't they?" said Dosser. By now, George was serving someone else further down the bar. I could hear him saying "Oh yeah?" to my explanation as he walked away, but I knew he hadn't taken it in.

I looked over at Dosser. "Automate it?" I queried.

"Yeah, you know. Like Fords or something; 'ave robots do it an' all that."

I hadn't given it much thought really. It seemed like such a bitty job that I wasn't sure a robot could do it. I was always adjusting things and checking the die and poking scraps of metal out of the way and fiddling with the blowers that blew the parts out of the back and all the rest of it. I couldn't imagine how a machine could work a machine like that.

"I don't see it, somehow," I said to Dosser.

"Future," he said. "It's all gonna be fucking robots soon. By 1984 they reckon."

"Bollocks," announced Dibby, arriving at the bar with two empty pint glasses in his hand. "Two 'ere, George," he ordered, putting the glasses down on the bar between us. Just then, Jim the contractor and Irene, his tarted-up wife, came in and edged behind Dibby, making for the dartboard.

"All right, Dibby?" asked Jim.

"Can't grumble, mate, can't grumble," answered Dibby. " 'Ere, Brian, smell this." Dibby pulled a ratty-looking cigar from his sports jacket and stuck it under my nose.

"I can't smell a thing, Dibby . . . this cold."

"You still got that? Christ, you want that amputated, you do. Look," he said, pointing at the cigar with his plump finger. "Fuckin' Cuban, ain't it? Mike Riffle gave it to me today. I'm building a patio for 'im — 'ere, you seen 'is daughter lately?"

"What, Rosie?" asked Dosser.

"Yeah," said Dibby. "Bristols like fuckin' torpedos, mate!"

Dibby put his hands out in front of his chest, made a bouncing motion, and smirked.

"She's a kid," I pointed out.

"So?" challenged Dibby.

"What's that one over there?" asked Dosser, nodding toward the girl in the green pullover. "What . . . seventeen?" he guessed.

"Dunno," said Dibby, "go an' ask 'er, shall I? George? Two lager 'n' limes 'ere, mate."

"All right, Dibby, all right," grumbled George, leaning over and picking up the glasses.

"You should do somethin' about that cold, Brian," he said as he pumped out the lager.

"Yeah, yeah," I mumbled, pulling out my wallet. "Three pints here, George." Gary Glitter droned on in the background.

After another pint, Dosser and I sidled over to join Dibby and Fred Box for a game of shove ha'penny. Dosser gave the girl in the green pullover a look as we edged by her table, but she just made a small face and carried on chatting with her friends.

On the shove ha'penny board, Fred Box was dusting some powdered chalk over the wood, getting it smooth for a game. After we'd had a few shots, I became irritated by the chalk dust and let out an almighty sneeze. The white powder flew up everywhere, especially on Fred's new bomber jacket.

"Jesus, Brian, look at my jacket! Can't you do something with that nose?" he complained, brushing the chalk off.

"Yeah, like 'ave it taken off," Dibby recommended.

"Right," said Fred, still frantically swatting his jacket.

"I've taken Lemsip for months, aspirins, Vick inhaler — even tried some of that herbal muck Sharon got from the health food store," I said. "Nothing's affecting it."

"You'll 'ave that till next year if you don't see a doctor or somethin'," warned Dibby. "And when you do go, tell 'im to take a few inches off it, will ya?"

They all had a good laugh at my expense. Dibby was a fine one to talk: he had thinning blond hair, a round, ruddy farm boy's face, little red lips, and a great fat hooter. My nose, it was true, was biggish, but Dibby's was even bigger. I pointed this out to him with a raise of my eyebrows.

"At least it's not bunged up all the time. Fuckin' 'ell, Brian, I'm surprised you can breathe. It's a wonder you don't die in yer sleep with that nose," said Dibby, preparing a coin for a shot.

"What's the score?" he asked Fred.

" 'Ow should I know? I wiped all the markers off when I cleaned the board after Krakatoa erupted 'ere."

"New game, new game," demanded Dosser, nudging me. "Last one's null an' void, then, right?" We were losing, as it happened, so he was happy.

"Yeah, yeah," said Dibby resignedly.


On returning home from the pub, I attempted to creep up to the bedroom. Unfortunately, at the bottom of the stairs, I couldn't suppress a rip-roaring sneeze and banged my head in the dark. I heard Sharon groan and, realizing I'd disturbed her, gave up the tiptoeing bit and clumped up the stairs. The next morning, Sharon had bags under her eyes and was well irritable. She fried up some bacon and eggs with a lot of banging and clacking down of plates while I sat at the table blinking and letting my nose stream into a hankie. The bright lights in the kitchen were making my eyes water, and the first cigarette really got me sneezing. Outside the rain was turning to snow and you couldn't see the sky for it.

"They forecast this, didn't they?" I said, pulling my mac on.

Sharon was silent and handed me my sandwich. Before I put it in my lunch box, though, I couldn't resist opening the foil and having a look at it. Without thinking, I bent my head down and took a sniff. Returning from the living room with the cat in her hands, Sharon stopped dead.

"Why," she queried, "are you sniffing that sandwich?"

"I dunno," I replied, looking down at it. "Just wanted to know what it was, that's all. Just curious like."

"Curious? Curious?" She opened the door and dumped the cat outside. "Well, why don't you just lift the bread and take a bloody look. Or better still, bloody well ask me! Why sniff it?"

"I didn't wanna spoil it," I answered lamely. "I mean, the bread looks crumbly, it might fall apart if I open it—look, I don't bloody know. Just thought I'd sniff it, that's all. And you don't seem to be in a talking mood, so I didn't want to bother you with asking like."

"Not in a talking mood?" she said, really uptight now. "Not in a talking mood? Oh no, it's all right for you. Half a dozen pints and you sleep like a baby! It's *me* that has to suffer your bloody great nose all night! *I* have to listen to it! Moaning and groaning you was. Snoring and breathing through your mouth—sounded like a train up there, you did."

"Yeah, well, call the doctor, then, all right? Quick, before I go. See if you can get me an appointment around lunchtime."

"I will," agreed Sharon, her dark mood relenting a tad as she picked up the telephone and called our local GP.

"You've got a cold," declared Doctor Garnet, pulling his stethoscope off. I didn't know what to say. He'd been poking around for five minutes, shining lights into my ears and eyes and stuffing that lollipop stick down my throat. Now he tells me this?

He fumbled around with a piece of paper and scribbled out a prescription for antibiotics. A complete waste of time. I'd take them for a couple of days maybe and then give up because you're not supposed to mix them with alcohol.

Doctor Garnet was virtually useless. He was too old to be practicing, in my opinion; all he ever did was write out scripts for antibiotics. And his young partner—this Indian geezer who smelled funny—all he went on about was smoking, drinking, and lack of exercise. Nonsense, really.

"Give up smoking and cut down on the beer, Mr. Porker," he instructed when I saw him last summer. And I'd gone in with a strained wrist! But he couldn't just look at the wrist—no, he had to give me a thorough physical and then he tells me to give up my only pleasures! Always a waste of time, seeing a doctor.

I picked up the antibiotics at the pharmacy and swallowed a handful as soon as I got back to work. I reckoned I'd better stuff as many down as I could before the evening. It was Friday and I've got to go to the pub on the weekend—got to.

Sharon was mildly pleased that I'd seen Doctor Garnet, but when I said I was going to the pub, she went livid.

"Brian, you know those antibiotics don't work if you mix them with booze! You're not going!"

"No, no, no, darlin', it's all right," I pleaded, already getting my mac on. "I'll drink that—what do you call it? You know? Kaliber. That nonalcoholic stuff."

"Nonalcoholic? What, you?" she demanded incredulously.

"Yeah."

"Don't give me that bollocks!"

"Sharon, honest," I whined. "Look, it's the darts match tonight. I'm playing with Dibby. They're expecting me, all right?"

"No, it's not bloody all right!"

She was clenching her teeth and going red, following me into the kitchen where I was already opening the door. It was windy outside and snow was still in the air; they reckoned on more over the weekend. I blew a monster sneeze into my hand and left. As I walked down the narrow concrete path on the side of the house, I thought I heard Sharon let out a scream.


I was in bed, sometime in the early hours of Monday morning, having this dream about walking through an unknown town, holding a stalk of asparagus, and pointing it at people. I don't know why asparagus, because I don't think I've ever eaten it unless it was in a Chinese takeaway. But it seemed to have a great effect on people when I pointed it at them: they backed away from me, looking very nervous.

Right in the middle of this dream, just as I was pointing the asparagus at a young woman, I felt like I'd been smashed in the face. A blinding red light flooded through everything. I screamed, thinking we were being attacked by an intruder. I had a silly thought that it might be Fred Box and Dosser, because me and Dibby had thrashed them at darts on Friday and beaten them at shove ha'penny on Saturday, even though they were better than us at both games.

A monster pain gripped my face and I leapt out of bed, smashing into the chest of drawers and knocking over the bedside table and light. I put my hand to my nose. It felt wet and warm and funny. I plunged into a panic, yelling "AH-AH-AH" as the pain became so intense, I thought I was going to die.

When I finally located the light switch, I reeled like a drunk at the site of blood on my hands. Looking in the mirror attached to the chest of drawers, I saw that my face was covered with blood, and where my nose had been, there was just this weird mess and the lower half of my nostrils. That was it: only the lower half of my nostrils was left, little flaps of skin wiggling around with blood oozing above them. My nose just wasn't there anymore. The next thing I knew, I was outside in the snow moaning and staggering around.

Some neighbours heard the commotion and ran out of their homes to find me bouncing off parked cars and kicking the snow, looking for my nose. Though near dawn, it was still dark and my car was gone. I couldn't figure out what had happened to me; I just knew I wanted my nose back.

"Do you know where your nose is?" asked the doctor as he inserted a needle in my arm. "Because there's a chance, Mr. Porker, that we can reattach it if we find it in time." People in white bobbed around me, and the white-tiled ceiling above my head spun crazily. There was a gap in my memory: one minute I was flailing around, cursing like a madman, the next I was on a gurney immersed in blinding light. I knew the man who had asked me the question was a doctor by his Indian accent and white gown. But I couldn't answer him; I couldn't think clearly enough.

The silence was suddenly broken as a man in blue barged though a swinging door that I vaguely perceived in my peripheral vision.

"We've found the nose!" the police officer shouted. "It's on its way now!"

I was so out of it I didn't know what he was talking about, but I found out later that Sharon, who'd driven off with the car and my nose, had taken the Cronwell round-about too fast and gone into a skid. She'd got stuck in a snowdrift on the edge of the road. Luckily, a police car was in the vicinity and the cops had spotted her car; the officers had noticed red splashes on her clothes and found a ten-inch kitchen knife on the passenger seat, covered with blood. She was hysterical but managed to explain that she'd thrown the nose out about a mile back just outside the White Lion Pub.

"What nose?" the police demanded.

"My husband's nose!" she screamed.

They sped off to look for my nose and discovered it sitting in the snow right on the edge of the White Lion car park.

Officer Tolby was the one who found it. I used to go to school with him. He was quick-witted and knew how to handle the situation: he told his partner to call the hospital, and they turned up with a box of ice to collect the nose. Later, Officer Tolby said he wasn't sure that Sharon was my wife, but he had a funny feeling that he recognized the nose.

"Never forget a face," he said later in court, " 'specially the nose." It was Tolby who insisted I press charges against Sharon, calling the incident "a heinous criminal act." In fact, he was so concerned with my welfare that he visited me twice in the hospital and once at the plastic surgeon's, where I was finally lucid enough to provide a statement.

After the operation, which was a complete success, I returned to my home to find a cold, empty house devoid of Sharon's personal belongings. The TV set, cooking utensils, and several items of furniture were also missing. Sharon had gone to live with her mother and I was left with nothing but the bare walls to look at, and my new reflection in the bathroom mirror. I lived this grim existence for three months, barely venturing out except to buy food and beer. And then we went to court. . . .

"In my experience," said Doctor Halifax, a noted psychologist called in to testify against me, "this kind of spousal abuse is quite common. After years of severe irritation, the victim experiences a sense of helplessness and feels that the only resort available to them is to remove the offending instrument of irritation—in this case, the nose. I've seen cases where a wife or husband's superior intellect has become, in the eyes of the victim, something that is used to belittle the less intellectual partner to the point of continual embarrassment. We might see an instance where the partner, continually degraded and made to look unintelligent—especially in the company of friends or strangers—decides he or she can no longer take these attacks and cuts off the aggressor's head, the head being, in this circumstance, the object that degrades and demoralizes the victim to the point where he or she feels no other act will relieve them of this constant punishment."

Vicki Hobbit, a vicious, frizzy-haired woman Sharon had hired to defend her, pressed the doctor for more damning details. "And so," she announced with much dramatic flair, "would you consider that the defendant had reached a point of helplessness due to the continual aggressive behavior of her husband's sinuses and his negligence in correcting their extremely negative effects? That she felt no other course open to her, and in a moment of what could

be considered 'temporary insanity,' due to the constant bat
tering she received from her husband's nose, lost control
of her normal disposition and thus removed the offending
organ?"

"This would appear to be the case, yes," agreed Doctor
Halifax.

"And could this constant battering be compared, in
your opinion, Doctor, to an act of rape?" prodded Hobbit,
repeating an assessment she had used many times during
the course of the trial.

"It might be an apt comparison, Miss Hobbit, yes,"
stated Halifax ominously.

I had hired John Cadwell to defend me. He was a local
solicitor of good reputation. In his austere oak-paneled office he had appeared supremely confident and pretty much
assured me of victory. In the courtroom, however, he
seemed to crumble at every argument put forward. Miss
Hobbit had rounded up more experts to testify in Sharon's
favour than he had anticipated; the "temporary insanity"
angle she employed was working well, and I was getting a
real roasting from everyone called up. Outside the court-
house, women's rights groups began turning up, brandish-
ing banners that said OFF WITH THEIR ORGANS and NO
MORE WIFE BATTERING, along with other aggressive slo-
gans.

Dibby and Dosser came to my aid, of course. They
lied through their teeth and said I'd only drunk nonalcoholic beverages in the pub that weekend. But George, the
bartender, insisted that I'd drunk Younger's Bitter. He even

described to the court the way I had joked about the antibiotics and how they were going to be "pissed right through my system."

Sharon did a lot of crying and immediately got the sympathy vote, saying how I'd had this bad nose ever since we'd been married and never tried to do anything about it. The most disturbing part of the whole affair was that after the prosecution showed them a picture of me blind drunk at some Christmas do at work—before the mutilation—the jury couldn't stop staring at my face in a most alarming manner. They could see that my nose actually looked better now. In the photograph, my snout was as red as a postbox and I looked like an emaciated W. C. Fields.

And the funny thing was, my sinuses had really cleared up. Cutting off my nose had killed that cold stone dead. And I could smell better than ever. Plus, my nose was smaller and the scars—according to a noted plastic surgeon—could be covered up with skin taken off my behind. Everyone seemed to think I'd come out of it pretty well, considering.

"That night, Brian was snoring so loudly, and I'd slept so little lately, that I was beside myself and lost all control," offered Sharon in her final testimony. "So I went downstairs and got the kitchen knife, but I can't remember thinking about it or anything. It was like something else had control over me: I just sort of snapped and it was like looking at another person doing it.

"Then I found myself outside, holding the nose and

the knife. I had no idea what I was going to do. So I just got in the car and drove. When I found myself outside the White Lion, I stopped and looked at the nose and then flung it out the window. I felt glad to be rid of it. That's the last time that thing pokes around in my cooking, trying to find fault, I told myself. That's the last time I'll have to hear him talking in an irritating, thick voice where every word begins with the letter D. I felt relieved when I saw it lying in the snow, bleeding. He's hurt me with that nose for far too long."

And then, of course, she broke down and cried. I felt the jury scowling at me, and Cadwell looked morose. What really tipped the scales in Sharon's favour was Hobbit's relentless use of the rape comparison. I complained to Cadwell about this ridiculous argument after it was all over — after they'd found Sharon not guilty. But he seemed resigned to the verdict and actually agreed that it really *was* like rape, when you thought about it. I didn't even know you could be done for raping your wife — after all, you are married to her. What was *that* all about?

None of my mates at the White Lion understood this argument either, but they had plenty of laughs about the whole thing.

" 'Ere, you got yer nose up yer own arse again, Brian?" was the first thing Dibby said the night after the bandages were removed — after the skin graft operation.

"Eh, your face favours fart, mon!" shouted Fred Box, who was well up on Jamaican slang.

"Yeah, yeah, all right," I said. But I had to see the humour in it, and after a few pints, I was cracking up with the rest of them.

"Oi, Brian," said Dosser as I took a long swill of bitter, "get your bum out of that glass! What, gonna take a shit in it, are you?"

"Likes to fart in his beer first—gives it a bit of flavour!" shouted the big-breasted girl in the green pullover. But I reckoned she fancied me a bit, what with the new slimline nose and all. I'd gained a fair bit of notoriety, too, and that's always good for a bloke. For the first time in ages, I really felt like picking up that old bass guitar and having a go again, maybe even getting a little band together. Dibby used to be a fair old drummer when he was a kid, and I knew the landlord at the Black Swan might let us do a gig or two—all we needed was a guitarist and we'd be well away. Why not? We'd probably pull in the crowds out of curiosity. No point in wasting all that fame. No point at all.

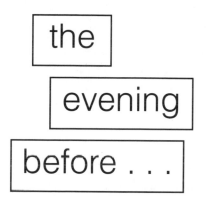

the
evening
before . . .

Kreska and her husband, Dander Smith, were having dinner with my girlfriend and me one balmy Friday evening in our Chelsea loft, six floors up, in a monolithic building that once housed printing presses but now crawled with alleged artists, rich Eurotrash, and punk rockers like myself.

The property had been purchased by an effete Lugano socialite two years before, and its cavernous, raw-space floors had been divided into units replete with massive industrial radiators, metal pipes the size of a man's chest, and rolling, wavy ceilings built to withstand the enormous weight of the presses. Where once those presses had hissed and boomed and squirted ink, now the muffled strains of house, rap, and punk rock rumbled through the pipes, and lovers' quarrels in Italian, often fueled by cocaine—the building's drug of choice—could be heard echoing in bathroom vents at all hours of the night.

The four of us attacked a seafood gumbo and guzzled Pouilly-Fumé, our voices accelerating in volume as the drink took hold and Kreska's spike heels tapped on the maple floor in a jagged beat. As soon as the dinner (which, although delicious, was merely a preliminary for the real dish) was finished, Dander pulled out a gram of Peruvian, light on the mannite and zero on the speed, and the mirror and sterling silver straw became our launching pad into those noxious heights of egocentricity so typical of late-seventies evenings. We enthused about our latest projects and guffawed over Stephen Stills's legendary steel nasal implants. We motormouthed about our own teeth as if they were a highly important topic.

As the night sped forward and Dander's Peruvian diminished accordingly, I offered up some Tribeca nonsense with a serious glass-splinters burn to it, just to keep us honest. Dander and I talked of doing a record together, which I, in sobriety, would never consider, him being an over-producer of the worst type. The women moved over to the couch, where they discussed the latest, most ridiculous hairstyle of one of the building's more famous occupants, and began laughing so hard, I thought they would cough up blood.

It was then that I remembered the Evening Before Pill. The Evening Before Pill had come to me, like many gifts of dubious merit, backstage at a club gig in New York, roughly a week before. There, my band and I, the Debilitators, had given a ripsnorting performance to a packed house of rabid, leather-clad lunatics whose sole reason for being at the show—it appeared from my view on the stage—was to project streams of beer and spittle into my mouth and to damage themselves severely either with substance abuse or the now-quaint ritual of mass pogoing.

The postshow backstage scenario was de rigueur for the period: hordes of liggers packed into a tiny graffiti-daubed dressing room, chain-smoking, guzzling white Boucheron or beer, popping into the toilet in pairs only to reemerge chattering like wind-up toys, grinding their teeth as if plugged into the mains. It was within this parodic tableaux that the surgeon appeared as if from nowhere, hovering with an out-of-date Medusa hairdo, inches from my face.

"Hi, I'm Doctor Allfox!" he said forcefully, and I assumed that the exclamation mark was, in fact, a legitimate feature of his name, as normal as a Nordic umlaut.

"You know what happens next," he went on, his nostrils dilating like black holes in space. "You have to keep doing the coke till dawn, even though you feel like dogshit."

"Right," I mumbled.

"Ever feel like going back to that first line of the evening—the one that worked? You know what I mean?"

I knew what he meant all right. The junk was addictive and everyone seemed to be on it. In those days, even your accountant would come backstage and offer you a hit. The wretched coke craze raged through the music industry like a mutant virus, infecting every level with jived-up superficiality, squeezing the talented, the talentless, the stupid, the intelligent—the whole gamut of the rock 'n' roll firmament—into a narrow band of jaw-breaking banality.

In a way, we all became equal: you would think nothing of spending an entire evening in garbled, meaningless conversation with utter greaseballs who at the time seemed to be your friends, your bosom-buddy confidantes with whom you would no doubt be tight for a lifetime. As long as their supply didn't dry up.

But at that time, nobody had any sense. We just wanted to keep on going.

"Yeah," I said, looking up at the wild-eyed Allfox! "It would be great to be able to take something that just . . . I dunno . . ."

"Takes you back to the beginning of the evening?"

"Exactly!" I said, seizing the idea with enthusiasm. "So that you could start again, 'cause, you know, after four or five lines, you're not really enjoying the shit anymore, you're just . . ."

"Going through the motions? Doing it because you hate the crash?"

"Yep. Uh . . . what was your name again?"

"Doctor Allfox!"

"Right, right. What kind of doctor are you?"

"I'm a surgeon. And by the way, I'm a huge fan of yours. I always play your stuff when I'm operating. Do you ever feel like cutting people up? I mean, listening to your music, it sounds like you would."

I looked up at Allfox!, taking in the hawklike nose, the glassy, obsidian eyes, and the Afro hair that resembled that freak at the party in *Midnight Cowboy* who has a single line: "My hair is like tendrils, they reach into space."

Allfox! was obviously a psychopath, but under the influence of three lines, half a bottle of Boucheron, and a couple of hits of grass, he seemed like a pleasant, likable chap.

I explained to him that, no, I hadn't really had the urge to cut someone up but saw no real harm in his unusual peccadillo—providing the intensity of my music didn't force any mistakes from the Allfox! scalpel or its volume wake the hapless patient in the middle of a heart bypass.

"By the way," he said, his voice dropping and his birdlike gaze flicking around the throng to either side of us, "I've been working on something. A drug that'll do just what we've been talking about. A pill that will take you back to the beginning of the evening. Want to be in on its development?"

"Wow," I muttered, which he appeared to take for a "yes."

"Yeah," he continued conspiratorially, and suddenly it seemed that Allfox! and I were in our own bubble removed from the thrum of chatter in the room. "Got a couple of boffins working on it now. Couple of rogue chemists. They did a nice little THC replicant last year. Wanna try a little?"

"Rather!" I exclaimed foolishly.

Allfox! pulled out a folded scrap of a page from *Playboy*

right there in a room full of people, but no one seemed to notice. Unfolding the paper, he revealed a heap of beautiful mauve powder. This stuff looked tempting enough to rub all over, and when he handed me a Biro top, I didn't hesitate in scooping up two nostrils full. Where I had removed the powder, I noticed a tit staring up at me and I grinned at the doctor. As soon as the gear hit my sinuses, it wiped out the effect of the poor-quality coke I'd ingested earlier and *bang!*—I was stoned as a twit.

"Nice," I said, believing this to be a profound utterance.

"Right," said Fred, for that was indeed Allfox!'s Christian name.

"So," I said, trying desperately to hang on to the memory of what we had discussed moments before, "what about this other stuff?"

"If you're interested," said Allfox!, pulling out his card, "call me tomorrow, it's almost ready for a test hop. They're getting close, just need a few guinea pigs."

With that, the mad surgeon made for the door and the party came crashing back in a big dread wave.

The next morning I phoned Allfox! and over a nose-candy meeting he enthused about his chemists—Heckle and Jeckle, he called them—and how close they were to perfecting the Evening Before Pill. A few field tests to get the bugs ironed out and they'd have a perfectly marketable product on the street in no time.

"Bugs?" I ventured.

"Well . . ." he hedged. "You know: pill shape, colour. The time it takes to come on. Nothin' to worry about."

All he required from me was to recommend the product to a few well-connected rock 'n' roll business clientele whose voracious appetites for toot would ensure, Allfox! reckoned, instant success.

"Great!" I exclaimed, the nose-candy talking. "I'm in!"

"This is such an honor. I'm a huge, huge fan of yours," said the intense surgeon, smoothing his pale green hospital gown and lurching off to Surgery. Allfox! left me in his white office, wondering what the hell I'd gotten myself into.

And so, on that balmy summer evening, with Dander and Kreska giving each other little looks that suggested they make a speedy exit and the clock edging toward two A.M., I bolted to the German mahogany cabinet in the gloom of an alcove and quickly pulled out the vial of Evening Before Pills that Allfox! had couriered over the day before. And even though these people bored the living crap out of me like so many others on so many ancient nights, I didn't want them to go. If they left, there would be little excuse to continue overindulging, and I was determined to bore them with a video of a performance by the Debilitators at an obscure Essen kino; besides, Dander had at least another gram and a quarter left, whereas my Tribeca nonsense was down to a few measely shards.

The producer and his wife were not going to leave my girlfriend and me chewing out the insides of our cheeks and slugging bourbon in a futile effort to attain unconsciousness. Oh no. We were all going back. Going back to about eight in the evening, when we still felt fairly human, before our descent into the hoglike beings that now inhabited my cavernous Manhattan loft. Back, back, to that clean, anticipatory state, fresh of nostril and pink of tongue and ready to whack up white dusty train lines from a polished mirror through a sterling silver straw.

"Ah . . . Kreska," yawned Dander, delicately trying to pry the girls apart with none-too-subtle body language. "It's . . . ah, closing in on two A.M. I'm a little wiped," he said with a mock stretch.

"Wait!" I almost yelled. "We got to check this out. A doctor gave it to me."

I spouted on enthusiastically about the benefits of the product and without too much arm-twisting managed to convince the three of them — even though Dander halfheartedly waffled on about a mixing session the next day at noon — that the Evening Before Pills were well worth a bash.

Out came the Smirnoff and we each washed down one plain white tablet, returning to the dining room table to await results.

After about fifteen minutes miraculous changes occurred. We began, as one, to feel revitalized, straightened, normalized, unplugged in. Incredibly, that foul, thickened feeling of too much coke, booze, and tobacco was being erased at awesome speed; that normally irreversible experience of overstressed synapses, slurred speech, and the god-awful density of what felt like a pair of leather trousers where the lungs used to be was decaying at a breathtaking clip. And then—as Allfox! had promised—we found ourselves back at the beginning of the evening! Of course, the clock still inexorably hurtled toward dawn, but the four of us no longer had the weight of hours of overindulgence in our systems.

Out in the street, car horns still blasted as people drifted from the Limelight to Danceteria; in the corridor, a door clicked shut and a laughing couple headed for the elevator. Would we use the Evening Before Pills as a universal hangover cure while the night was still young? No, we would not! *Whoopee!* we yelled. We can start all over again!

But then, as Dander gleefully pulled out his coke and reached for the blade and mirror, something very odd began to overtake our senses.

We didn't stop there.

We kept going right on back!

Within minutes, our internal clocks, which moments before had clearly been signaling that before-coke anticipation, now indicated that before-dinner-first-glass-of-wine feeling.

It was at this point that I began to feel a sliver of apprehension as I perceived that we were indeed, as one, experiencing the same thing.

"Do you feel . . ." I ventured, as yet another metabolic

cycle flooded through me. But I never finished the sentence, and with frightening acceleration, I was back at lunchtime, the blood-sugar level of that meal reversing and the hangover of the night before inching its way into my brain and gut.

"Oh dear," gulped Dander as the results of Thursday night's bender at the Milk Club hit him like a curse, and before we knew it, the four of us were draped over the furniture as we plummeted through the wee hours of Friday morning, back into the drug and alcohol stupor of Thursday night.

Outside, the traffic swelled to its usual Saturday morning volume and we slept on thickly.

We woke up backwards and retraced most of the week in the space of a few hours until finally we found ourselves ready for a late breakfast on Tuesday morning. Most of the week had gone . . . the wrong way.

Well, I had some excuses to make. I swore I would get Allfox! and apologized to my girlfriend and our guests for this outrage; at the very least, the mad surgeon would eat humble pie and his boffins would be warned of the terrible chemical bungle they had unleashed.

Dander and Kreska finally left, albeit with somewhat stunned expressions.

"Nice . . . ah . . . nice dinner party, man," Dander commented sheepishly as I showed him the door.

"Yeah, long night," I said. "Listen, Dander, I'll get that bastard doctor."

"Right . . ." he muttered, and I rushed back in and called the hospital.


"Yeah, sorry about that," said Dr. Fred Allfox! almost nonchalantly. "Uh, what day is it for you?" he asked, sounding distracted.

"Day? What fucking day?" I hissed. "Christ, I dunno. Tuesday, I think. At least that's what it feels like. We had sushi Monday night and I can still taste it when I belch — always repeats on me, sushi. Look here, Allfox!, what went wrong? It's slowed down, thank God, but I'm still going back a tad here."

"Don't worry, it'll stop pretty soon," said Allfox! blandly. "You know these genius underground chemists. They don't tell you much. I think they left out a step in the process. The stuff came out, like, a molecule short or something. Or a molecule too many. I think that was it. Happens all the time in drug development. Anyway, listen," he went on, "tell your friends I'll call them and apologize. I wanna talk to that Dander, he ruined the last record by the Bloody Cavities. Overproduced the shit out of it."

"Right, right," I sighed, looking at my watch as the taste of bagels and lox from Tuesday's breakfast crept across my tongue. It was just after noon on Saturday.

"Anyway," Allfox! continued, "the boffins know there's a problem, they'll brew up another batch by next week. I'll test it out and give you a call. I gotta run now. Gotta take some poor bastard's leg off—or was it a brain tumor? Shit, I can't remember, got my days all mixed up. I'm sure I'll figure it out when I get in there and get the Debilitators cranked up, heh heh. Know what I'm saying? Catch ya later . . ."

With that, Allfox! hung up. I could imagine him in a blood-spattered gown in the operating theater, leaning over some unfortunate with the scalpel floating betwixt brain and kneecap, my vicious songs bouncing around the white-tiled room as the surgeon tried to make up his mind. Allfox!, a wild gleam in his eye, unsure of what day it was.

I never heard from him again, which was okay by me. And that white devil cocaine gradually slipped out of the pop music world and found its logical niche as crack, burrowing down into the substrata of society; right down there with the poverty-stricken blacks and Hispanics, leaving them to dream of the Evening Before Pill. Who knows, maybe Heckle and Jeckle got the formula right and it's out there now, being sold as a chaser to the little vials of rock. I'm not that interested anymore. A pill that could take you forward? Hm, there's a thought . . .

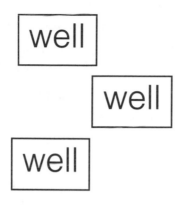

They bounced down my drive and across the wooden bridge in an old blue van that had HOW'S YOUR WATER? painted on the side of it. Gadafucca and his dad got out as I opened the front door and went up to greet them, barking orders at my dog, Bowser, the mad rottweiler. I had to watch that dog. I'd picked him up at the pound a couple of months after I'd moved into the house and had to discipline him with an iron hand. He loved me, for some reason, and I'd chosen him because he was the only animal in the pound that didn't go berserk as I walked between the cages inspecting the dogs. He just sat there, cow-eyed, following my movements with great interest. I realized I'd made a mistake as soon as I got him out of there when he dragged me halfway down the street. The previous owner, according to the pound keeper, had dropped Bowser off with one simple piece of advice: "Just put him down — he's no good to anybody." I was told this *after* I had agreed to take him.

Naturally, I didn't want the dog to tear a hole in my well-driller's leg on our first meeting, so I shouted, "No bite! No bite!" as Bowser leapt toward Gadafucca with his eyes bolting out and his fur up. Once Bowser had gotten used to somebody, he was okay, unless I told him otherwise. Then, with little prompting, he'd lurch into attack mode and I reckon tear a man's arm out by the roots. A hell of a guard dog, that boy.

Vinny Gadafucca was short and built like a side of beef; he wore a faded Harley-Davidson T-shirt, one size too small. His father had a trick knee and limped after him, darting his black eyes around the property as he adjusted a weird-looking black hat that perched on his small bald head.

"Hey, Vinny Gadafucca. How ya doin'? This is my dad."

I shook Vinny's hand. It felt like a beat-up leather punching bag. His dad nodded cautiously.

"Big ole dog," said Vinny's dad, eyeing Bowser.

"Got him at the pound," I said. "He's all right, gets excited at strangers, don't you, boy?"

Bowser rubbed my leg and I ruffed up his black fur as we made our way up the hill behind the house, getting straight down to the business of looking for a good site for the drilling.

"Somewhere around here?" said Vinny, pointing to a heap of flat rocks that caught the sun in the meadow.

"Well, that's the snake pit, actually," I said, trying to act casual. "Lot of snakes live in there. I like snakes. How about further up?"

I pointed up the hill about fifty feet, just at the end of the lawn where an old logging path ran through the meadow and into the forest that surrounded the grounds.

"Snakes?" asked the old man, limping back a few paces.

"What kinda snakes?" questioned Vinny nervously. "Garter snakes?"

"Yeah, just garters and green snakes. Found a big water snake in there last year, under the rocks, and a good-sized milk snake showed up recently. You know, I just don't want to disturb this bit, that's all." Saying this embarrassed me because most of these country people had no time for wild-life—especially snakes. In their book, the only good snake was a dead one.

"Don't like snakes," said old man Gadafucca. Then he launched into the usual horror story that local guys carry around with them and haul out like a bad fishing tale when anyone mentions reptiles.

"When I was workin' in the machine shop, just after the war," said the father, "big ole black snake came right through that front door and across the floor and I saw it and I swear, it got right up there and put its head up ready to strike! We all got the hell out of there, I tell you!"

It was no use pointing out that black rat snakes aren't poisonous. Every local I'd dealt with was ready to believe that this part of upstate New York was infested with hostile, venomous snakes lurking in the timber, ready to kill anything that moved. Recently, a guy with a backhoe stopped by to turn over a piece of land where I planned on starting a vegetable garden. As soon as the subject of snakes came up, off he went with his bit of nonsense: walking through some bushes one day, he felt something jab his arm and a couple of red dots appeared on the skin and his arm blew up like a balloon. The hospital diagnosed it as a "puff adder bite." "Yep," he said, scratching his gnarly chin, "ole puff adder got me."

I was just some rich yuppie from the city, I wasn't going to lord it over the locals by handing out free herpetology lessons, so I just nodded and looked concerned, not mentioning that he'd have to go to Africa to get bitten by a puff adder.

With the vicious serpent tales put to rest, we picked a suitable spot for drilling, and Vinny went over the figures with me, emphasizing that just because other wells along the road were only two hundred feet deep, it didn't mean mine was going to be.

"Could be anything," he growled, looking around the property. "With water, you just don't know."

"What about one of those guys with the birch sticks? Those water diviner guys?" I was uneasy with Vinny's vagueness; I knew that with well drilling, you pay by the foot.

He brushed back his short, curly black hair and creased his little mouth. He seemed like the type of guy who would punch someone out with the slightest provocation, and at the mention of water diviners I could see him bristling.

"Water diviners? Ah, those guys . . ." Vinny appeared disgruntled at the mention of dowsers and began to inform me of their many failures. Desiring to appear manly and not some hippie-dippy crystal-gazer, I joined him in a bravado guffaw and we let the matter drop.

Vinny said he'd be down with his son tomorrow, bringing oak beams to shore up the bridge, just to be on the safe side, the truck weighing in at about eighteen tons. On the following day, if they could finish the job they were currently on, they'd start drilling.

We walked down the hill with the old man in the lead, prodding the ground with a branch to balance his gimpy leg, giving the snake pit a wide berth. Bowser, saddled with a remarkably short memory, came tearing through the orchard on the other side of the house, barking at the sight of the men. The Gadafuccas quietly climbed into their van and left.

It was a bright clear day with a hint of autumn in the air. I strolled over to the snake pit and lifted a rock; I hoped to get a glimpse of that milk snake again. "They can be ugly," the man with the backhoe had said.

Tilting back a big rock, I watched four or five garter snakes slithering off. The largest one I grabbed, holding it gently until it calmed down. I liked the big ones; they relaxed quicker than the smaller specimens and were less prone to releasing their foul, musky defense odour. Within minutes, I had the snake crawling over my hands as calm as a pet.

I marveled at its fluid, thick-set body, its yellow longitudinal stripes, and its interlocked, keeled scales. I held the snake up to the blue sky, examining its unblinking eyes and flickering tongue before releasing it among the rocks.

There were timber rattlesnakes in the mountains, and copperheads, too, but they were scarce; and despite the dread that the mention of these species produced in the locals, most people would come no closer to a poisonous snake than a *National Geographic* TV special.

The abundant wildlife inhabiting this part of the country was, in fact, one of the reasons my wife and I had purchased the property. We'd had enough of our apartment in Brooklyn, its noise pollution, insane parking problems, and dangerous subhumans of every stripe. She liked deer, I liked snakes. And this piece of land with its meadow, old apple orchard, and mountain forest had plenty of both, plus great bird-spotting opportunities and the occasional bear as a bonus. Then my wife decided to leave me for a burly mechanic and moved back to Brooklyn, just like that. Couldn't handle the quiet of the country, she claimed. Or my brooding over my career — or rather, lack of career. My depression would have been devastating if it wasn't for the outlandish success of a jingle I had recently composed for Wendy's and the offers of work that followed. Both Burger King and the old Hamburglar himself had been on the phone to my newly acquired agent, and this excitement had kept me sane in the deafening silence of the mountains, which was even beginning to get to me. Just a short time ago, before we'd moved up here, I'd been a struggling keyboard player, working with a bunch of loser jazz musicians in an upstairs lounge above a restaurant in Little Italy that was widely suspected, due to its longevity and utter lack of clientele, to be a Mafia front. Now I was on a roll with this fortuitous jingle gig and I wanted to plow money into my property before my wife filed for divorce and claimed the lot. Dealing with the vagaries of men and their big machinery was not my forte, but I was determined to handle it like an inhabitant of the real world instead of the avant-garde musician I really was. I had to admit, though, that I was beginning to feel as stressed out as I had been in the city.

It was two days later when Vinny drove the huge drilling rig over the bridge. I watched with trepidation as it thundered past the house and up the hill, leaving big, muddy tire tracks in the lawn. Clouds were building and serious rain was expected for the next few days. I glumly imagined the mess this operation was going to make on my land.

As he cranked up a deafening generator to power the rig, Vinny gruffly introduced me to his son, Bud, who was taller than Vinny but just as stocky. Bud barreled around in ill-fitting blue jeans and a dirty, tight white T-shirt, barely acknowledging me through his wire-framed spectacles. I tried a few pleasantries, but the pair seemed uninterested in small talk, preferring to concentrate on the frightening-looking derrick-type affair that they hoisted above the spot where the drilling would begin.

I felt nervous and wimpy as the thick-set Italians yelled at each other over the noise of the generator. They did tough, manly things with items of heavy machinery that I didn't understand. As the clouds opened up and a steady rain began to fall, I backed away casually and left them to their task.

Inside my house, the stone walls reverberated to the incessant drone of the generator; loud crunching and squealing noises boomed down from the hill as the drill bit bore into the rock-riddled earth. It was impossible to ignore the noise, which was augmented by the deep buzzing of the pump in the kitchen that drew water from the stream fifty yards away. I silently cursed the previous owner for not getting a well drilled himself; he'd lived in that house for thirty years and had relied on an ancient concrete well. Now I was stuck with the problems of a clapped-out pump that drove me crazy. I had ruined the thing by leaving a hose running for two days by mistake and, according to my plumber, the pump's impellers were now worn out. This accident was the final straw with the stream water, which was tasteless anyway due to the purifying ultraviolet light system it ran through. I had to do the right thing: get me a drilled well like everyone else.

By midafternoon, I was frustrated that the Gadafuccas

had not silenced their brutal machinery and rushed down to the house, triumphantly announcing that they had hit water. Reluctantly, I edged outside into the rain, trying to look nonchalant. Vinny had assured me that his firm wasn't the type to "drill for money" like some outfits, that when they hit water and got a good vein, they'd stop. They were honest guys, according to him, unlike the shysters who operated in the region, many of whom routinely drilled an extra hundred feet in order to rip off the townies who had been flooding the area, snapping up the choice properties for weekend retreats.

As I sidled up the hill, I was shocked to see the edge of the meadow, all the way down to the drainage ditch that fed the stream: it was thick with brown slurry, rolling down like volcanic lava. My heart sank when I saw that the rocks of the snake pit were practically covered with the muck; and as I walked by the pit, I spotted two garter snakes crawling over the soaking lawn toward the house, thick streaks of slurry embedded in their scales.

Even worse, some of the bigger rocks had been tossed further into the meadow so as not to impede the progress of the slurry; it seemed to me that the snake pit had, in fact, been demolished, probably about a half hour into the well-drilling operation.

I stomped up to the work site, irked at the behavior of the insensitive brutes who continued to yell at each other as they straddled a huge pipe of metal casing and lowered it into the hole. But what could I say? They'd treat me like some artsy-fartsy pansy if I started whining at them. This was big, manly stuff they were doing, and the slurry was only conforming to the laws of gravity.

Clearing my throat, I yelled over the din of the generator, "Eh, all right? How's it going, guys, need coffee or anything?" I felt like a woman, asking if they wanted refreshments, but they ignored me as they jiggled that rusty casing down into the hole. Once they'd got it submerged, Bud grabbed his shovel and flailed at the slurry, directing it down the hill. Vinny, covered in mud and oil, hustled past me as if I wasn't there and buried his head in the generator, taking a wrench to it. I stepped up behind him, huffing my chest out, assuming a casual yet tough pose in the rain. "Any water yet?" I asked lamely.

Finally, Vinny pulled his head out of the machine and strode past me a second time toward the drill hole, this time acknowledging my presence: "We're down three hundred and we just hit bedrock!" He joined his son, hacking away at the slurry that continued to boil out of the ground in thick, churning coils.

I slunk back to the house, a feeling of impotence coursing through my blood. Even with my scant knowledge of well drilling, I knew that you have to bore through bedrock to get to the water, and they'd gone down three hundred feet before they hit it? That would cost me at least double what I'd expected — probably triple!

I stalked around the house, getting a headache from the noise, staring aimlessly through the windows toward the stream, watching the rain come down in sheets. Abruptly, with a descending roar, the machinery quit and Vinny's son Bud trudged down to the house. "Can I borrow your phone?" he asked brusquely. I handed him the cordless phone and he punched a number.

"How far ya down?" I boomed in a manly way. But he started shouting at someone on the phone, ignoring me completely.

"How far are you down?" I repeated, trying not to sound like I was pleading.

"Three hundred and fifty," he replied, and turned away. "Be back tomorrow. Need some dynamite."

"Dynamite?" I questioned the thin air, for Bud was already gone.

It was late the next afternoon when Vinny rolled down to the house and knocked on the door. I'd gone up the hill a few times that day, keeping a distance, checking the progress, listening for explosions.

"Well, we got water. Not a lot—'bout three gallons a minute—but we got it," said Vinny, not looking too happy.

"Three?" I queried, knowing that wasn't great.

"Yeah, dumped some explosives down there to open the veins. I guess we could keep drilling, but we're down a ways now," he said.

"How far?"

"Five hundred and sixty."

"Five hundred and sixty . . . feet?"

"Yeah, way down below the bedrock. Water tastes good, though—no sulfur anyway."

I felt a tingly helplessness under my skin; I'd hoped for 200 feet and gotten 560. It was going to cost me. Had they been "drilling for money" after all? And what could I do about it, drop a tape measure down the hole?

"Goddammit, I need a shit," announced Vinny, suddenly jiggling on the spot.

"Oh sure, come in," I offered.

"Ah . . . nah, I'll just go up in the woods." He turned and headed off toward the forest.

Up at the drilling site, Bud continued to direct slurry away from the lawn.

"Kinda deep," I said to him.

"Yep," said Bud. Apparently, this guy was in a permanently aggravated state and none too familiar with social pleasantries. He seemed thoroughly put out with the work, but I imagined he was too dense to get much enjoyment out of relaxation, either. Vinny emerged from the forest and I wondered what he'd used as toilet paper.

"Here, taste it," he said, passing me a black tube that snaked from the depths of the drilling rig's machinery. I cupped my hands and drank a little. Surprisingly, it was drinkable — not sulfury, but maybe a little metallic.

"Looks like the blasting opened the veins as much as they're gonna go. Now we gotta bomb it with chlorine and put the pump down," Vinny said, washing his boots with water from the tube; I never saw him wash his hands.

"Okay, great," I heard myself say, but I was thinking about Vinny crapping in the woods like a bear.

"So, once they've dug the trenches, you'll lay the plastic pipes around the lines, right?" I was attempting to sound businesslike. Vinny had agreed to install the pipes to protect the lines from shifting underground rocks, a precaution my plumber had suggested. Now he looked sullen and his son bristled and snorted, but I was determined to make him stick to his promise.

"Yeah, yeah," he mumbled. "We'll lay the pipes."

"Okay, then," I said, dying to get away. "Uh . . . they're digging the trenches tomorrow. Christ, I hope this rain stops."

"S'gonna be a mess," said Vinny, glancing at the sodden ground. "Anyway, we'll get your pump down for you now—you seen it? It's a real high-tech baby."

"Uh . . . yeah, I've seen the brochure," I lied. No way was I going to hang around while these jokers dangled an extremely expensive and complicated piece of machinery 560 feet down a hole, attached to God knows how many miles of delicate electrical cable just waiting to be shafed and shredded against that rusty casing. I couldn't bear to watch, so I hurried off to the house to brood and drink tea.

About an hour later, I was out throwing a stick for Bowser when I heard an earsplitting yell. Vinny was sprinting up the hill toward the cabin of the drilling truck. Bud was staring at his hand, cursing. Blood poured down Bud's arm as his father scrabbled in the truck, emerging with an oily rag. He quickly wrapped it around Bud's hand.

"Finger!" Vinny yelled as they sped past me to their van. Bud looked ashen and shocked. Noticing the blood ooze through the cloth, I figured he'd somehow got his finger caught as they'd been lowering the pump—probably lost it, judging by the look on his face. But the next afternoon, I thought I was dreaming when Vinny and Bud appeared and began threading wires through a hole in the top of the casing. I didn't like to stare, but I couldn't see a bandage or any sign of injury for the life of me, and the pair of them stormed around, snipping away with wire clippers and dismantling the rig in their usual aggravated state, as if nothing had happened.

Meanwhile, the trench diggers had arrived with the backhoe and were ripping up my beautiful land, turning it into a churning mess of mud. I winced as the rain pelted down. If it didn't let up soon, the flooding would be of Biblical proportions. Jack, the backhoe owner, stood next to me as the driver of his angry yellow vehicle began ripping up rocks and mud with the jaws of the digger.

"I'm sure that kid lost a finger down the well yesterday," I said, pointing to Vinny and Bud as they pulled plastic pipes out of the back of their van.

Jack followed my gaze and made a face. "These guys are animals," he said, as if that explained everything.

Somehow, by late afternoon, the backhoe reached the house without bringing thousands of gallons of rainwater with it. I was in the crawl space discovering, to my utter disbelief, that the builder had poured eight feet of concrete in the very corner where we had planned to bring the lines through. Vinny, Bud, Jack, the plumber, and myself stared into the hole at the end of the trench, gazing in silence at the deep concrete footing.

Various suggestions were made as the miserable wind whipped rain into our eyes, but none of us seemed willing to take on the task of breaking a hole in the concrete. After a while, the plumber, another stocky Italian, pulled me aside and said, "You know what's happening here, right?"

"What do you mean?"

"No one wants to take on this thing. It's like, that couple of feet between the outside of the house and the inside is like no-man's land. Who's responsible for doing it? Know what I'm saying? You got eight feet of concrete inside and God knows how deep it goes—know what I'm saying?"

"So . . . what do we do?" I asked, watching the other guys pull away from the trouble spot, washing their hands of it.

"You better get on the phone," advised the plumber. "You better see if you can get a jackhammer over here to smash through it, s'all I can think of."

"Christ."

The men knocked off work and went home, leaving my land looking like a mudslide whilst I plowed through the Yellow Pages, searching for the word "jackhammer."

The following day, after a massive Polish guy armed with the requisite machinery had punched a hole in the concrete, Vinny, Bud, and Vinny's dad turned up, closely followed by the plumber and Jack. I was astounded when I noticed Bud's hand was wrapped in a heavy bandage with a finger pointing straight out, like it was in a cast.

"Hey, Jack," I said to the trench foreman. "Look at Bud's hand . . . I don't get it."

Jack lit a cigarette and took a deep pull. "Animals," he muttered.

After gimping around the place for a while, old man Gadafucca drove off in the van with Vinny, leaving Bud to thread the well lines through the plastic tubes, which he did in a surly manner, hating every minute. The plumber was under the house installing the water tank.

When the van returned, I presumed it was Vinny, so I didn't bother investigating; I spent my time watching TV, trying to ignore the general commotion. Then Bud came to the door, all red-faced, huffing and puffing. Really pissed off.

"Listen," he said. "My ole man's got a bad back and he's on another job. I should be helping him. It ain't our job to lay these plastic pipes down, the trench digger should be doing it—we're going, he can do the rest!"

Incredibly, there was no bandage on Bud's hand. I couldn't see a scratch on it! I suddenly got mad. I didn't know what this joker was playing at, but I'd had enough of it.

"Your dad's your boss, right?" I demanded.

"Yeah?"

"Well, he agreed to lay those pipes, so get the hell on with it! That's part of the deal, it's paid for, pal. No one else is doing it, okay? I've had enough of this shit. Just 'cause you hate your fuckin' job ain't my problem. I want it done by today so I can get this crap wrapped up. It's gone on for days longer than I expected and I'm gonna get a bill from you people that I'll have to take a mortgage out on. So do me a favour, huh? Honour the goddamn agreement!"

120

Bud looked at me; I could see the dim wheels turning in his head. For a moment, I thought I was going to cop a big ham-sized fist on the nose, but he gritted his teeth and sort of wobbled in front of me.

"Uh . . . okay," he said tonelessly. "But my dad needs his lunch, he's over on Van Huen Road. I gotta take him somethin'. And I want your autograph—you got any photographs?"

I felt my head jerk back and my eyes bug out like a cartoon character. "Photographs? Uh . . . no. No, I don't think so."

"You're the guy who wrote that Wendy's song, ain't you?" demanded Bud, referring to my jingle.

"Well, hardly a song, really. It's just a—"

"Yeah, well, I hear it all the time and Wendy's is my favorite—here, sign this." Bud delved into his pocket and produced a grubby bill from the local hardware store, which I obediently signed. With this utterly surrealistic (I had *never* been asked for my autograph) scenario behind us, I attempted to regain my former dander.

"Where's your dad?" I demanded.

"He's drillin' by a trailer home up the end of—"

"Right, okay. I'll take him his lunch, you carry on working, all right? What's he gonna want?"

Bud described an elaborate hero sandwich.

"Right, I'll pick one up and take it to him, okay?"

"Okay," said Bud, giving me an angular look.

He went off to the trench and I shut the door with a sigh of relief. I searched around for my car keys and wallet,

121

but before I could make an exit, Jack appeared, looking flustered.

"What's up?" I said, seeing his concerned expression.

"The Italians!" he exclaimed. "They're fighting in the ditch!"

"Italians? I thought Vinny was on another job!"

As I followed Jack up the hill, I noticed the van in the drive and remembered it had returned. Bud must be fighting with his gimpy granddad, I thought. But when I arrived at the trench, I could see two heads bobbing over the ridge of mud, going at it like boxers. As I looked into the trench, I saw two thick-set men wrestling in the sludge, both wearing similar dirty white T-shirts, both with spectacles and mud-coated blue jeans. Both men looked exactly like Bud! They were identical, except that one had a bandage wrapped around his right hand with one finger stuck straight out in an attempt to avoid further injury from the conflict.

"What the . . ." I stammered.

"Hey, guys!" yelled Jack. "Hey, guys, cut it out, will ya!"

They looked up at us through their steaming wire-framed spectacles and then they got right back at it like knives, wrestling, kneeing each other's groins, and trading insults. In the flash of a synapse I thought of Bowser, the mad rottweiler, and with two claps of my hands I summoned the brute from his slumbers in the kennel and set him on the Italians. The animal leapt into the churning mud and began gnashing at their filthy trouser legs. Down went the twin with the damaged digit, flat on his back in the muck, his arm stiff in the air like a flagpole. The other clown was flailing insanely at Bowser's head as the crazed beast tore into his muddy rump.

The desired effect achieved, I ordered the dog to desist, hoping his severe training would now pay off.

"No bite! No bite!" I implored, and amazingly, the animal drew back sharply and scrabbled from the trench, plonking his sopping hindquarters at my feet, tongue lolling and lungs going like bellows as he surveyed his captives. Without a word, the lads got up, pushing and shoving each other, and went straight back to work, cursing like navvies, as if nothing much had happened.

"Nobody said a thing to me about identical twins," I said to Jack as we walked away.

"Animals," he mumbled.

I found Vinny on Van Huen Road attending to his drilling rig, which was backed up to a shiny new trailer home. He stood up painfully as I pulled in, his leathery face wincing.

"Hi, Vinny, got you a hero. I told your boys to keep workin', then they had a fight. Is that normal?"

"Ah . . ." he groaned, rubbing his spine. "Goddamn back. Those boys? Jesus, they come out fightin'. From the moment they was born they was fightin'. Nice sandwich."

The sun was breaking through the clouds for the first time in days as Vinny tore into his sandwich. For a fleeting moment, a woman's face appeared in the window of the trailer, then drifted off into the darkness.

"So . . . which one hurt his hand, Vinny?"

"What?"

"Which one of your boys hurt his hand?"

"Mikey," he said, working his teeth around the steak, onions, and peppers. "Lost his goddamn finger. Forefinger — right off at the joint."

"Mikey."

"Yep."

He turned around and started shoveling the slurry that was just beginning to ooze from the well hole. I noticed that he wasn't drilling on a slope, as if he wasn't expecting too much slurry; as if he wasn't expecting to go too deep. A guy came out of the trailer home dressed in a ratty checked shirt and a faded Yankees cap: a shallow well for the locals and a deep one for the city folk, I was thinking.

"See ya," I said, and drove back home.

Mikey and Bud were just packing up when I got back, thumping each other all the way down the hill. Granddad Gadafucca had turned up to have a nose-around and followed them, making a little face as he limped past the demolished snake pit.

The backhoe had filled in the trenches, leaving sickening swaths of mud that obliterated most of the lawn at the back of the house. Jack and his driver left, followed soon after by the plumber. At last I was rid of the lot of them.


About three days later, after the chlorine had cleared the system, I had good clear water and plenty of it, so I decided to celebrate with a bottle of wine and a hot bath. I ran the faucet and watched with satisfaction as the water filled the tub. I undressed and immersed myself, placing a glass of Chianti on the side of the tub.

It was dark and silent outside as I lay in the bath stewing, drowsy from the effects of the wine and warm water. I fixed my blurry eyes on the pale green wall tiles, dimpled with condensation. Languidly, I shifted my vision to the crinkly ceiling plaster, where witches on broomsticks and evil faces came in and out of focus.

The water in the tub cooled a little, so I turned on the taps, mixing just the right amount of hot and cold, pulling the plug to release old water and make way for the new. I lay back and took a sip of wine, staring at the water, which gushed in a perfect mix from the big chrome faucet. Abruptly, there was a splutter, and a hiss of air issued from the spout. The water continued running, then spluttered again, this time more violently, making a clanking sound in the pipes behind the tiles. I groaned, wondering if it was just air in the pipes or some larger problem, when in the midst of a jet of water, something fired out of the faucet like a bullet.

I watched it bob around the eddies of the soap bubbles, spinning back under the tap water torrent only to bob out again and spin in the greenish swirls. I leaned forward and turned off the taps, then reached into the water to locate the mysterious object. It brushed past my fingers like a piece of old soap, but I failed to catch it.

I lay back in the tub again and there it was, bobbing

up from under my back and, finally, floating in front of my nose. I delicately picked it up and stared at it, giving the thing a few exploratory squeezes.

It was about an inch long, purple and spongy; it had one ragged end with something hard poking out of it and one smooth end with a dull, flat disc attached. When it dawned on me that it was Mikey's finger, I almost threw it across the room. Instead, a fascination gripped me and a mischievous idea came into my mind. I smiled and gently placed the macabre object on the edge of the tub.

The next day Vinny came around and we sat at the dinning room table going over the bill. As I suspected, it was three times as much as I'd hoped, but what could I do? I'd been present the whole time. I'd watched the casing go down. The Gadafuccos seemed to have used the amount of casing they claimed. So I pulled out my check-book, tore off a check, and handed it to Vinny. As soon as he'd looked it over, he hurried to the door, saying he had another job to get to.

I was about to close the door behind him when I remembered the finger.

"Hey, Vinny . . . wait up, I got something for you." I turned and raced into the bathroom where the finger still sat, wrinkly and purple, on the white edge of the tub.

"Here you go," I said, placing it in Vinny's saddlebag hand.

"What's this?"

"It's your son's finger . . . Mikey, or Bud, I forget."

"Mikey's finger, for Christ's sakes?"

"Yeah, I caught this big ole garter snake yesterday under the rocks — four, five feet long. Longest one I ever saw.
Whilst I was holding him, he started coughing — really
retching up, you know? So I put him down on the grass,
and he heaved up this here finger. Do you think it's too
late to reattach it?" I said.

"Jeez," said Vinny, staring at his son's purple finger in
the palm of his hand.

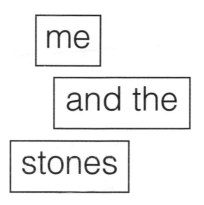

# me
# and the
# stones

The news came as quite a shock to me. I'd just gone down to the Indian store on Westbourne Grove to pick up a pint of milk and some bread for toast when the headline on the *Daily Mirror* displayed in a rack of papers across the road outside the newsagents caught my eye: MICK JAGGER DEAD, it screamed across the rain-soaked street.

Everything around me went into slow motion, and for some reason I just stood there, outside the Indian store in the rain, watching a little Irish vagrant about ten years old shuffling up and down near the newsagents, begging for money. He wore a filthy old raincoat about two sizes too big and had a mop of thick, wavy black hair. His colourless trousers flapped around his shoes and his face was greyish, like the sky.

The boy hustled up to a fat old lady who was heaving a tatty wicker shopping bag toward the zebra crossing, but she just ignored him and carried on, plodding over the black and white stripes on the road like a mutant chess piece. The kid trotted off again past the newspaper rack, his eye on a couple of Iranian gentlemen. MICK JAGGER DEAD, trumpeted the headline.

I walked into the Indian store, blinking at the bright array of products stacked from floor to ceiling, and went to the refrigerator for a carton of Lord Raleigh's milk. The shop smelled like old vegetables and detergent; I could hear the rain suddenly get heavier as I paid for the milk.

Crossing the mouth of Hereford Road, I quickly stepped onto the zebra crossing on Westbourne Grove, making a taxi lurch up behind a double-decker bus that stopped dead in an oily puddle with a huff of air brakes. The pungent smell of olives emanating from a nearby Greek deli caught my nostrils. As I approached the news-agents, the Irish kid sniffed and fished around in his pockets, then made a beeline for me.

"Give us ten p, mate," he said in a surly manner.

"Piss off," I snarled, not looking at him but transfixed by the headline on the *Daily Mirror*.

"You fucker!" he exclaimed, and I had to stop myself from turning around and clocking him. I'd gone through exactly the same routine countless times on this corner. Once, I'd delivered my standard rebuttal to a group of four of the little tykes and they'd followed me for a while, shouting insults. At times like these, I felt like I was in a Dickens novel and often considered selling my flat to move to a more upscale area, like St. John's Wood.

I hate the *Daily Mirror*, but for some reason bought it, ignoring the more staid announcements of Jagger's death in the *Independent* and the *Times*.

MICK JAGGER DEAD, barked the headline in thick three-inch type.

I stuffed the paper into my plastic bag along with the milk and dashed through the rain into the Greek deli, where I picked up some pita bread and taramasalata, deciding on a more exotic breakfast than toast. Then I headed back home.

Climbing the stairs to my second-floor flat, I could feel the dampness of the rain on my hair and the dampness of the walls in the building merge. Once in the flat, I put on the kettle, made some tea, and heated up the pita bread in my decrepit old gas oven. The cracked paint on the kitchen walls registered briefly, as did the thought of having someone sand them down and repaint them. I stared at the crumbs on the old lino floor and vaguely thought about pulling the Hoover out, but decided instead to eat my breakfast and read the Mick Jagger article.

"Mick Jagger, the wildman singer for the pop group the Rolling Stones, died last night after being run over by a bus on the Kings Road," it said.

The fifty-five-year-old Jagger was out with Michael Sutton-Prell, the essential oils magnate, and Lady Hamilton-Strout, the real estate heiress, on a binge-up in Chelsea, when Jagger fell into the path of a Number 58 double-decker bus. The threesome had just eaten at Qui!, the trendy new French restaurant on the Kings Road, and consumed two bottles of expensive red wine. Mark Szvitzgal, the Royal photographer, had been with Jagger earlier that evening and said that the singer was already "half cut" before his dinner engagement. Witnesses say Jagger had been smoking cannabis earlier that day.

Sutton-Prell said that Jagger was telling a joke about the Dalai Lama and a hot dog vendor when he stepped back off the curb laughing, lost his balance, and fell under the wheels of the bus.

I dipped my pita bread into the plastic container of taramasalata and digested the rest of the article: it recapped the Stones' infamous sixties escapades, their importance in rock history, and, of course, offered lots of dirt on Jagger's love life. Most of these statements were inaccurate in typical *Daily Mirror* fashion, even to a casual observer, and I wondered if the whole thing was a hoax. But sure enough, when I turned on the radio, various stages of the Stones' and Jagger's turbulent lives popped out of practically every channel, save for Radio 4, which featured a segment about a man who lowered microphones into the weed beds of ponds to listen to the weeds grow whenever the sun came out. The man spoke with an amusing whistle that squeaked out at the front and end of certain words, like some bizarre cleft palate punctuation.

I listened to the crackling weeds and imagined the sun

breaking through the windy clouds over a dark pond in Surrey. Then I dialed in a pop station and listened to more details of Jagger's accident and further Stones trivia.

The next day, I had to go to New York to record a song on a tribute album that commemorated the death of some black guy I'd barely heard of. The producer said he could send the tape over to England if I preferred, but I sensed a free flight in the offing and told him I'd do a better job in New York. The morning of the flight, I sat in the back of my sixties Vanden Plas, driven by my occasional chauffeur, Bindhi, and read more trash in the *Mirror* about the Stones.

Bindhi, a Pakistani, kept me informed about various developments in the Indian restaurant business. He was a bit of a pop buff, too, and drove for other rock stars. He often filled me in on the gossip that was doing the rounds: who Chrissie Hynde was screwing; how the gutter press had a deal with Cliff not to reveal his transvestite tendencies; how Millionaire Paul Young and his Model Wife weren't getting along very well—little tidbits like that.

Normally, I would have no truck with talkative drivers, but Bindhi was always informative and entertaining, so I kept him on.

"Terrible about Mr. Jagger, sir, isn't it?" he remarked as we sloshed toward Shepherds Bush in the driving rain.

"Yes, Bindhi," I agreed, looking up from my paper and studying his brown neck above an immaculately pressed white shirt. His jet-black hair was neatly cut and never showed so much as a trace of dandruff, and he wore a light cologne that didn't accentuate hangovers the way some of that junk did.

"They're looking for a replacement, I hear, sir. Keith insists the Stones must roll on. Do you think they'll find someone suitable, sir?"

"Jesus Christ, you're kidding?" I exclaimed, not having heard or read this piece of remarkable information.

"Oh yes, sir. I work for Simon Beauvier-Froid sometimes—you know, the rubber baron?"

"Oh yeah, friend of Mick's, wasn't he?"

"Keith knows him, too."

"Really?"

"Oh yes, sir. And I drove Mr. Beauvier-Froid to his helicopter pad on top of the Sussex Building yesterday, you know. He was on the phone in the back of the car and I heard him talking to Keith in New York."

"Yeah?"

"Oh yes, sir. Mr. Beauvier-Froid was saying, 'Oh my goodness, Keith,' and such like, sir. 'You can't be serious, Keith. You're going to be looking for a replacement for *Mick?*' "

"You're shittin' me, Bindhi!"

"Oh no, sir. He was using my cellular phone—his was stolen in a Chelsea wine bar the night before—and I get an instant computer readout on my phone and that was Keith's number all right. I know Keith's number, sir."

"That's the stupidest thing I've ever heard, Bindhi. What do you think?"

"Well, I don't know, sir. A very hard post to fill, sir. A very hard gig that would be. Oh sir!" he said brightly as we peeled off the M4 toward Heathrow. "Maybe they'll consider you for the job!"

Bindhi and I had a good laugh at this, but I felt a weird thrill shoot through my gut. After all, what musician hasn't fantasized about being in the Stones? They practically wrote the book.

After completing the tribute song, I stayed on in New York, padding around my loft in Tribeca at all hours, recording new songs on my digital 16-track. Most days I would walk around the Village or Soho, eating lunch in as many diverse establishments as possible in order to glean inspiration from the city's extraordinary denizens.

So long as I didn't visit a bar and piss away the day, I usually had the building blocks of a song rattling around my head by early evening, and after a light dinner that often consisted of a couple of containers from Balducci's or Dean and Deluca, I'd start hammering away on the guitar or piano and begin to knock something up for the tape recorder.

Late one evening, after about a month in the city, I was laying down a harmonica part on a rootsy little number when the red light on the phone began to blink. I stopped the tape and stepped out of the padded confines of my small recording den, walking in near-darkness to the blinking red light.

"Hello?" I slurred, feigning tiredness in case it was someone I wanted to get rid of.

"Issat Brian Porker?" asked a croaky English voice.

My mind reeled through the possibilities but drew a blank. I scanned the dim loft space, hearing only the ticking of the massive industrial radiators that lined the opposite wall.

"Yeah?" I answered, still on my guard.

"It's Keith Richards . . . we 'aven't exactly met. I just wanted to chat with you. I've always liked your stuff, man."

Shit. I felt dizzy all of a sudden. One of the monolithic radiators let off a really loud ticking noise that sounded ominous. I gulped and fumbled in my pocket for a cigarette but came up empty handed. There was an ashtray on the table by the phone with a dog-end in it, so I pulled out my Zippo and lit it up, singeing my eyebrows in the process.

"Er . . . great," I said, feeling slightly nauseous from the smell of the burnt hair. But I made a real effort, not wishing to appear a complete prat, and managed to pull myself together. "How's it going, Keith? Sorry about the recent bad news . . . uh, I'm glad you caught me up, I was just workin' on some new stuff."

I felt really stupid saying this; the whole sentence seemed like such a dumbass thing to say.

"S'all right, y'know," said Keith, "just something you have to deal with, got to keep going, man, y'know?"

"Yeah, I know what you mean," I said, again feeling like a prize clown.

"Listen, Brian, can we, like, get together? I wanna pass something by you, y'know?"

"When?" I asked, feeling my pulse accelerate. Keith sounded a tad drunk; he was slurring a little, but from what I could gather, this was pretty normal.

"Well . . . uh, are you busy right now?"

"No. No. I was just, y'know . . . fiddlin' about, man. Nothin' serious. Shall I come . . . like, where are you?"

"Great, man, great!" he said. I heard a lighter click and a dull hollow sound like a half-empty bottle hitting a table. "Listen, man, I'll send a car, all right? What's your address?"


Inside Keith's brownstone on the Upper West Side, I sat down nervously on a huge paisley pillow affair in a dark, airless room littered with overflowing ashtrays, crumpled cigarette packs, and empty bottles of Rebel Yell. There were a couple of lamps draped with silk scarves and a small amp strewn with leads, broken strings, and more cigarette stubs.

Keith came in and I stood up and shook hands with him. He was dressed in black jeans and a black T-shirt and, to my surprise, was quite short, like myself. He seemed to have an unusually large head, though, and his face had more crags than a mountain range. A Marlboro hung from his lips. He smiled warmly but, in the manner of English people, didn't really make eye contact.

He walked over to a stereo near the large bay windows and fiddled with a tape. Moving with a rolling gait, all arms and shoulders, he managed to put the tape in, then came over to the beaten-up sofa that sat against the wall opposite the big pillow.

"You heard any of this?" he asked as the tape began and the unmistakable sound of the Stones honked out.

"No, not out for another month, is it? What's it called?"

*"Cloven Hoof,"* said Keith, reaching for a bottle of Rebel Yell and taking a slug. "I think it's a good fuckin' record. Mick was proud of it. Thank God we got all the vocals done."

"Right," I said feebly.

Keith offered me the Rebel Yell and I took a hit. As he passed it over, I noticed this big silver ring in the shape of a skull on one of his fingers.

We talked about the new Stones record, and he twitched a lot and lolled his head and hands about in an uncoordinated manner; he had very gnarly hands and big blue veins that rippled down his biceps like cables. A huge tin ashtray on the glass coffee table between me and him overflowed with thick ash and dog-ends, and as Keith gesticulated, I found myself eyeing it nervously, ready to leap, in case one of those big gangly arms swung down too close to it.

I was quite sure we wouldn't get through this little chat without him knocking the thing over.

"Check this out, Brian!" Keith enthused.

He leapt up and adjusted the volume, sending the ashtray spinning on the glass table. Then he returned to the sofa with a guitar that he'd pulled from the shadows across the room and began picking along with the track, a funky rockabilly number. The ashtray slowed down, but then Keith began banging the table with his knee as he tapped his foot in time to the tune, causing puffs of ash and a dog-end to fall on the glass.

As the song finished, he bounded up to turn the stereo down, this time hitting the ashtray with the bottom of his guitar, which made it spin counterclockwise, the opposite of its previous direction.

"Listen," Keith said suddenly, lighting up what seemed an endless stream of Marlboros. "Man, y'know, things 'ave to carry on with the Stones, and we've been auditioning a few singers. It's like . . ."

"Really?"

"Yeah, man, yeah. But . . . some of the people are like, y'know . . . just fuckin' sorta impersonatin' Mick. Know what I mean?"

"Right."

"Well . . . man. Look, I like your stuff an' I know you've said in print how the Stones were an influence, which is great! That's what it's all about, man!"

"Oh . . . well, yeah, y'know . . . uh."

"Fuckin' right. So, do you wanna give it a try, eh?"

Suddenly the door opened and a woman leaned in. Her blond hair hung around her face, but I couldn't see her too well in the dark. I presumed she was his wife, Patti Hansen.

"Keith," she said.

"Oh, darlin', this is Brian Porker. Brian, this is Patti."

"Hullo, Brian, nice to meet you. Keith, you've got to be up early for that meeting, remember?"

"Oh, shit! The lawyer thing, right. Yeah, all right, love, I'll be up soon, all right?"

"Okay, 'night. 'Night, Brian."

"Yeah, good night. I won't keep him up long!" I said, trying a touch of levity. She smiled and disappeared.

"Fuckin' lawyers, they always wanna do their shit first thing in the mornin'. I forgot about that. Anyway, are you interested, y'know?"

"Christ, yes!" I said without a second thought.

"We're rehearsin' in this big joint down in the meat-packin' district. Where the faggots 'ang out. Not far from that fuckin' great sanitation pier on the Hudson . . . near the Anvil and the Spread Eagle—all that shit. Mick woulda loved it!"

"Picturesque," I said, feeling weird when he mentioned Mick by name.

"Listen to this one, Brian. Check it out."

Keith again staggered over to the stereo and turned the volume up. I took some more slugs of Rebel Yell, not bothering to wait to be offered any more. "Custom Fanny," a really decadent tune, blasted out, sporting a typical killer Keith riff and an evil, languorous Jagger vocal. It was prime Stones, somewhere between "Honky Tonk Woman" and "Start Me Up."

The idea of singing this stuff made the hairs on the back of my neck stand on end, but as I sat there watching Keith slashing away on the guitar, I also felt quite silly. I was wearing a really naff pair of corduroy trousers, a ten-year-old striped preppy-looking shirt with button-down collars, a clam-coloured Marks and Spencer jumper that my mother had given me two Christmases ago, and some weird, black, toad-shaped shoes I'd had for years. Keith had on a pair of jet-black lizardskin cowboy boots. They looked like they grew from the bottom of his jeans. They looked like he might have slept in them. I felt more like a suburban bank clerk than someone about to replace the late Mick Jagger in the Rolling Stones, the Greatest Rock 'n' Roll Band in the World.

I gulped down more Rebel Yell, trying to loosen up my movements, attempting to make appropriate facial expressions. But my face felt like it was disintegrating and my lips seemed to be disappearing. I tried to groove my body to the music but couldn't shake a ridiculous, nerdy self-image.

"Shit! I've gotta make you a tape," announced Keith. He left the room for half an hour while I lounged around on the paisley pillow, trying to relax with the Rebel Yell.

I happened to glance up at the mantelpiece that framed a stone fireplace and noticed a small white dish with a rolled-up bill sticking out of it. Keeping alert for signs of Keith's return, I jumped up and examined the dish, which contained a residue of white powder sparkling dully in the dim light. I replaced the dish but for some reason held on to the dollar bill, which I fiddled with absently until I heard a sound coming from outside the room, at which I promptly stuffed the note in my pocket.

When Keith came back he held a cassette in his hand. He fumbled it into the tape machine, rewound *Cloven Hoof,* pressed a few buttons, and started playing the record again from the beginning, making a copy for me.

As the first song began, I felt the back of my neck burning; I expected Keith's old lady to come crashing in at any minute to complain about his staying up so late. But she never returned, and Keith and I listened to the new Stones record again, him slashing at his beat-up Gibson and me twitching and bobbing my head about. Another bottle of Rebel Yell seemed to materialize in front of me and we drank the best part of it while the tape played. I was desperate for a glass of water but didn't like to ask in case Keith went off to get it and never came back; it was four in the morning before the new Stones album finished playing.

"Well, I gotta get up for that meeting tomorrow . . . lot of stuff to go over, know what I mean?"

"Yeah. Must be a lot of stuff."

"Here," Keith said, lurching at the stereo and practically tearing the tape copy out for me. "Can you learn some of this shit by next Saturday?"

"Uh . . ."

"Don't worry about all the words, y'know? Just pick up what you can an' I'll 'ave 'em typed out for you at rehearsals, all right?"

"Oh, well. Right. Great, man, great. Yeah."

I took the tape from him and sort of reeled a bit as I stood up; the tension and the booze had got to me and somehow I misjudged the distance and bumped into the glass table. The giant metal ashtray went shooting straight off the edge all over the carpet, clattering as it bounced around against the table's leg.

"Buh . . ." I blurted.

A thick pile of ash spread out around the table leg, bumpy with stinking cigarette ends. Keith and I looked at each other, but he just shrugged it off. He had a warm grin and didn't seem at all mad about it.

"Don't worry," he said, leading me to the door. " 'Appens all the fuckin' time!"


The rehearsal space was this giant floor in a dilapidated building on Washington Street that used to be a meatpacking company. As I entered the blackened doorway, I could smell the decaying meat products mixed with the odour from the sanitation dumping grounds nearby. It was a grey September afternoon and seagulls were screaming in the sky.

What with the nerves and the stench, my stomach was doing a number on me, and I felt myself gagging as I walked into that cavernous space, spying the equipment across the echoing floor from what seemed like half a mile away.

It was a very long walk to that equipment; the hard clang of an experimental guitar chord, quickly abbreviated, and the harsh English of a roadie shouting instructions made my blood run cold. I saw a dark pair of eyes, feral and emotionless, flash out from beneath a spiky Keith-like haircut. The guitar made a crackling sound as a roadie fed a new cord into it.

"Try that, Ron," the roadie shouted as he thumped back to the amplifier.

Ron Wood struck a chord, then tried a lead riff that he fudged badly before saying, "Yeah, all right." He lit up a cigarette.

Charlie was sitting in grim lighting, adjusting his cymbals. A big black guy started playing a bass riff. Keith was nowhere to be seen.

Eventually I reached that rarefied area; I nodded to a fat roadie, who greeted me with a perfunctory handshake. The three musicians ignored me for a while, then Charlie looked up from his kit, his face like a skull, and said, " 'Ullo, Brian, I met you once before, didn't I?"

It was true: he'd come to a recording session of mine almost twenty years ago, but the producer, whom Charlie knew, failed to actually introduce us, so we'd never really met. After a few nervous pleasantries with Charlie, I caught Ron's eye and strolled over. Ron and I had actually met on at least three different occasions, and this day's encounter was no different than the previous ones. He shook hands, smiled, and said hullo but made no effort to acknowledge me as a fellow musician; I might just as well have been a roadie, a fan, or some peripheral character like a radio station technician or a record company executive's assistant.

The black bass player, with whom I was unfamiliar, was much more friendly and raved on about a couple of my albums. This made me feel marginally more relaxed, especially since the guy was one of the many who had had to fill Bill Wyman's place in the whole cliquey set-up. But I wasn't sure what to say to him, really. I didn't know if he was in the band permanently, on trial, or just a stand-in for rehearsals (I got the distinct impression that this would never be made clear to me until we were about to go on the road).

On the road! The thought made me shake in my shoes as I stood there in that lonely, echoing space and watched yet another roadie setting up a mike stand.

I tested the mike but was too scared to actually break into anything resembling a tune. Ronnie began hacking away at a blues shuffle, which was quickly taken up by the bass player and Charlie. I stood there like a lemon, fumbling with my lyric sheets and gulping my Evian water, nodding my head and trying to appear casual.

Ronnie played the guitar with a cigarette dangling from his mouth, proving that you can't actually smoke and play guitar at the same time. Charlie sounded leaden and way, way behind whatever beat Ron was attempting. And the bass player played with consummate professionalism, making him seem totally out of place.

This weird racket went on for a while and I just strolled self-consciously out of the way and let them get on with it. A roadie lit cigarettes for Ronnie so that he could keep on playing.

The jamming disintegrated after a while and a guy who identified himself as an assistant went around taking food orders. Another hour went by in which I tried to make conversation with the band but only succeeded in getting a rapport going with the fat roadie, and then the Chinese food turned up. Everyone sat around and picked at it morosely. I drank some tea. Ronnie downed pint after pint of Guinness.

Eventually, Keith turned up, swaddled in a dirty white fur coat and a black fedora with a feather sticking out of it. He gave me a fairly warm greeting but immediately started joshing with Ronnie, further enhancing the closed-in, cliquey feeling. Then he asked an assistant where the telephone was and disappeared for another hour whilst Ronnie, Charlie, and the bass player attempted more half-hearted jamming.

Keith came back with a roadie in tow, swinging a couple of bottles of Rebel Yell. Plucking a Gibson from its stand, he began riffing through one of the songs from *Cloven Hoof.* The others joined in, but it was difficult to tell exactly where in the song Keith was. He looked over at me with small, bloodshot eyes. I responded by cautiously sidling up to the mike, scribbled lyric sheet in hand. There was no sign of the promised typed-out lyrics, so I had to bluff a lot, trying to avoid imitating Jagger's mannerisms too closely.

I'd worn more suitable clothing that day: a purple suede jacket from Trash and Vaudeville, a black T-shirt, tight black leather pants, and a pair of black basketball high-tops. But I still felt like a bank clerk in fancy dress or someone in a talent contest.

Keith's guitar was loud and Ronnie was playing a godawful mess that cut through all the vocal lines, making it hard to retain any sense of rhythm. When I tried to shake my ass and groove a bit, I felt like a total idiot. The number crashed to an end and Keith immediately broke into "Custom Fanny," a number that would probably be the first single from the album.

Having thoroughly learned this number, I pulled off my jacket and began really leaning into it, attempting a few experimental struts up to Ronnie or Keith. Ronnie blanked me out totally, but Keith was smiling and grooving with me. I sang my guts out and thought I'd be hoarse by the end of the session, seeing as I'd been too nervous to get the vocal monitor sound right in the first place and had done nothing to correct it.

Five hours later, after many mysterious breaks for phone calls and much gulping of Rebel Yell by Keith and guzzling of Guinness by Ronnie, we jacked it in and Ronnie rushed off to jam with some band at CBGB's.

Keith sidled up to me, twitching and scratching, offering a little praise, but not as much as I'd hoped for. Then he dashed off to a waiting limo, saying he'd call me later; gathering up my lyric sheets, I walked out into the darkness.

I felt drained and numb as I lay around the loft that night watching TV. It was as if I'd lost some blood, as if I'd had an encounter with a vampire. I thought I'd done pretty good, but who could tell? There was just no communication going on between these people that I could make out, but still, Keith didn't give me the impression that he would audition other singers. Nevertheless, after hearing how crappy their playing was and visualizing the brick walls I'd have to scale before I became accepted, plus the unknown quantity of the public's reaction to me being in Jagger's shoes, I suddenly felt much less keen on the whole idea.

Then I thought of the money and brightened a little. And Christ, think of it: being in the Rolling Stones! Me! I had to get my attitude straight here. This was the chance of a lifetime and I knew I'd done well in the end; I knew my voice, at least, was up to the job. And surely, that was the important thing, the singing. All that image stuff had to be less than secondary now that these guys were in their fifties. Keith just wanted a singer who really had the chops for the job. Surely that was the main thing. There were more wrinkles in that rehearsal space than in an old-folks' home! Yeah, I had the gig, definitely . . . maybe definitely.

I was about to turn in when the phone rang. Nobody calls me at two A.M., so it had to be Keith. I took a long gulp of the wine I'd been nursing and padded across the empty floor to answer it. A radiator hissed and the turned-down TV echoed dully in the near-empty space. A siren went off outside and the elevator in the corridor *whoomphed* to a stop. I heard laughing as the people next door fumbled with their keys.

"Hello?"

"Brian, Brian, Keith here. I'm in me car, just near you, man. Can I stop by?"

"Yeah, yeah, Apartment 2A. Press the buzzer and I'll buzz you up. 2A."

"Uh . . . what street?"

I gave him the full address and he hung up. He sounded practically legless and I wondered if he'd gone off to join Ronnie at CBGB's and if they'd had a bit of a confab about me. I was worried about Ronnie's reaction; he seemed to have a lot of pull with Keith, and with Mick not around, those two were obviously the power base in the band.

Keith rolled into my loft, clutching a bottle of Rebel Yell that clinked against his big skull ring.

I led him across the empty space, wishing I had more furniture. As it was, there was just the futon in the corner and the couch in front of the TV; we'd have to sit together on the couch unless I pulled the uncomfortable metal chair out from behind the partitions in the recording area I'd set up.

I sat down on the couch and muted the TV; Keith

plonked himself down, too, passing me the Rebel Yell. I didn't want to mess around, so I got right to it. Keith looked like he might pass out at any minute.

"Uh . . . so, Keith," I said, feeling a cluster of saliva building on the back of my tongue. "Um, what do you reckon, man? Are you gonna check out anyone else, or what?"

Keith sighed and slugged on the bottle. He made a face and pulled at his thick grey-and-black matted hair. He blew out some air and lit a Marlboro.

"I dunno, Brian. It's like . . . everyone loves yer singin', y'know?"

"Oh yeah?"

"Yeah, it's great, man. 'Custom Fanny' and 'Hot Ringlets'—you got it down, man! And, and fuckin' 'Last Stop Is Nowhere,' man, you sing the balls off that one . . . the old stuff, too, man, great. Fuckin' great. But, y'know, it's the Stones I have to think of. Not just personal taste, y'know?"

"Yeah," I mumbled, feeling like a brick had landed on my head. One of the massive radiators mocked me with its hissing and the elevator closed and descended. Keith lurched forward, stubbing out his Marlboro in my tiny marble ashtray. He pulled another one out and lit it, hardly missing a beat even though he was weaving around.

"Uh, I think, though," Keith continued, "we gotta have a bit more, y'know . . . image up there, y'know?"

"Yeah."

150

"It's like you, y'know, you look all right and let's face it—we're all gettin' a bit long in the tooth an' all."

"Heh heh."

"Right, but . . . I think we might need someone a bit more . . . impressive. Not in the vocal department, y'understand. You've got that down, man, but it's tough out there, y'know? And I think we need a bit of a bigger . . . uh, bigger . . ."

"A bigger what?" I asked, at least intent on getting a really straight answer as to why I wasn't getting the gig.

"Well, y'know. You look good, you look good, man. But you know Mick, well . . .'e was quite—how can I put this—uh . . . well equipped. Know what I mean?"

"What do you mean? What, his moves an' all?" I asked, feeling about the size of an ant.

"Yes, yes. His moves, for one thing, but . . ."

"I mean," I added desperately, "I can work on it, y'know? I just have to relax a bit. I . . . I can get the old struttin' around bit a lot more natural. I just need to relax and . . ."

"Well, y'know . . ." said Keith. "It's not just that. It's like, in tight trousers Mick was, like . . . y'know? *Impressive* is what I'm saying."

I was at a loss for words; Keith was giving me the elbow because of the stature of my crotch. My dick didn't look big enough! At least, that's what he seemed to be saying.

I grabbed the Rebel Yell and took a deep pull. Keith followed me, looking kind of sheepish now.

"You mean . . ." I began.

"Yeah, Brian, I mean, man, I saw ya today in the tight leathers an' all and y'know, the chicks used to dig Mick onstage not only 'cause of his moves, but also 'cause the man 'ad a fair-size wad there an' shit, man, it's like show business right? We gotta keep that sexual allure—this is the Stones, right?"

"But . . . I've had no complaints so far," I asserted.

"Sounds like you might 'ave fucked some of the same women as me!" said Keith, and we had a good guffaw. That broke the tension a bit because before he'd said that, I'd felt like picking up the marble ashtray and whacking him in the head with it.

"It's like," continued Keith, gesticulating with his arms and brushing his lighted cigarette dangerously close to the couch, "you're up there in front of fifty thousand people prancin' around with the cameras up yer bum an' all, right? Well, that's when you need to be, like, larger than life. Know what I mean?"

"Yeah."

"Eh, you don't 'appen to get an erection when you're onstage, do you?" asked Keith.

"Um . . . not normally, no. I don't think so." I was reminded of an old Patti Smith interview, where she was telling some reporter about how many times she comes onstage. A real fucking likely story, that one. "No, Keith, I must say, no matter what the reaction, I don't find performing in front of people that stimulating."

"Um . . ."

"So who you gonna go for?" I asked, genuinely interested in Keith's idea of a replacement for Mick. "That thick-lipped twat from Aerosmith?"

"What?!" exclaimed Keith, and we cracked up.

"What about David Lee fuckin' Roth, then?" I asked, joking again.

"Ha ha ha. That prat?" said Keith. "Don't worry, Brian. I'm not gonna hire a fuckin' clown just 'cause 'e fills 'is trousers out—although Sammy Hagar called up!"

"You're kiddin'?"

"No, fuckin' Sammy fuckin' Hagar! We'll 'ave Robert Plant next!"

"Hey . . . how far off is that, then?" I asked.

"Nah, fuckin' screams all the time, that cat does. I'll get a fuckin' earache! I don't know whether I'm wastin' my time here anyway, y'know? Maybe I should call it a day. Just do my solo stuff, I dunno . . . it's just . . ." And Keith looked suddenly tired and haggard, like he was getting ready to sleep for a year. "It's just, Brian, the Stones is my life. Fuckin' 'ard to let it go."

"But the Stones is you and Mick, man—*was* you and Mick."

"Yeah. Yeah. Maybe . . . I dunno, we'll try a few more out. I ain't givin' up until I know I'm floggin' a dead horse completely. Listen, I'll be off, man—more fuckin' legal stuff with the lawyers in the morning, know what I mean?"

"Oh yeah, right. Got to be a mess."

"Yeah," said Keith. "Look, I'll give you a call, right?"

"Yeah, man, stay in touch. I've enjoyed singing with you anyway, and the new stuff is shit-hot, man."

"Take it easy, man," said Keith.

And with that, he shook my hand and lurched out to the elevator, disappearing into its white coffinlike confines, dropping back against its far wall as if he'd gone instantly to sleep, his thick hair cushioning his skull and his face sporting the famous deathly pallor.

"How was New York, then, sir?"

"Fine, Bindhi, fine. I got a lot of writing done — always stimulating, is New York."

Sleet was falling as Bindhi gunned the Vanden Plas into the tangle of traffic at the Heathrow roundabout. The sky was like a lead weight and wind whipped at the sparse sapling birches on the grass verges.

Bindhi had supplied a copy of the *Daily Mirror*. I studied the headline. It was the usual tosh: something about a teenage sex vicar and parish rent boys; Jagger's demise was old news and there was no mention of the Stones holding auditions.

"So, Bindhi," I said, finding scant pop star gossip in the tabloid. "How's Millionaire Paul Young and his Model Wife? Whose face is Chrissie sitting on and have they shopped Cliff yet?"

"Ha ha. Millionaire Paul Young and his Model Wife,

I believe, are preggers again. Everything's hunky-dory I hear, sir."

"Glad to hear it, Bindhi, glad to hear it."

"Oh, but sir, I hear that pooftah from Duran Duran has recently had a very bad case of brewer's droop, sir."

"Really?"

"Yes, sir. Can't get it up for toffee, I hear—had to go to a clinic. His Model Wife is threatening to leave him."

"You're shittin' me, Bindhi!"

"Oh no, sir, I never shit. You know me, sir, no shitting from me—it was all over the grapevine two weeks ago. But I can't remember which pooftah from Duran Duran, sir, they all seem the same to me—all that mock Keith Richards hair and mascara, et cetera."

"Know what you mean, Bindhi. I don't know a thing about that band apart from the singer's just another David Bowie impersonator."

"Oh yes, sir, those early records were simply bad Bowie. How they caught on I'll never know, sir."

Bindhi drove through Bayswater, dropping the odd piece of gossip and filling me in on the latest Indian restaurant info. I was especially pleased to hear that the Bombay Brasserie had gone under, but this jubilation was tempered by Bindhi's assessment that a lot more yuppie chinless wonders would now be invading my local, the Standard, filling up valuable tables and screaming at the waiters to make everything hotter.

"So, sir," inquired Bindhi as we swung past the top of

Portobello Road, "anything interesting happen in New York, sir?"

I thought about Keith's first phone call and my late-night meeting with him and the subsequent rehearsal, which had now taken on the texture of a dream — a dream where one is constantly searching for a foothold. And then the discussion later that night and the crunch of reality as I realized that me and the Stones were to be no more enmeshed than we were when I first heard them over thirty-five years ago. There would be no fantastic voyages into those impossible realms they occupied, no ecstatic strutting and massive adrenaline rushes, no dangerous exploits of androgyny and excess, and no elevation into the order of the semi-divine. It would remain forever a vivid, transcendental mirage in the mind of a thirteen-year-old boy.

I stared out at the driving sleet, mesmerized by its relentlessness.

"Sir?" said Bindhi. "We're home, sir. Didn't do too badly, considering the weather and traffic."

"Oh . . . sorry, Bindhi. I was just dreaming. New York? Nothing much happened really. The usual, y'know?"

For a moment our eyes met in Bindhi's rearview mirror.

"Bye, sir."

"Bye."

As I stepped out of the Vanden Plas onto the pavement, my eyes caught the flap-flap of a pair of ill-fitting trousers approaching. It was the Irish kid, walking toward me with his hands in his tattered coat pockets, his black hair plastered around his face from the rain and a shifty look in his eyes.

I tucked my head down and made for the front door of my building, but there was no avoiding him and his pace quickened to intercept.

"Can you spare ten p, mate?"

I stopped in my tracks and looked into the little guttersnipe's eyes, which I noticed were green but quite empty, devoid of enthusiasm, heartless. As I reached into my trouser pocket, a shimmer of current ran through him and he edged nearer. I pulled out a dollar bill, a crumpled, rolled-up dollar bill — the bill I had taken from a dish in Keith Richards' New York brownstone. For a moment, I thought about stuffing it back in my pocket. But instead I handed it to the kid; he plucked it away and held it up, studying it.

I watched the rain hit the note, and then started to move off.

"What's this?" he asked in surprise.

"A dollar," I said, "what's it look like? You can change it on Queensway."

For a moment I thought he was going to disappoint me and sneer or throw it right back. I remembered once giving a young Hispanic beggar a bag of returnable bottles and cans on Seventh Avenue and having the lazy bastard push them right back in my hands, even though a two-block walk to the supermarket would have brought him a buck and a half.

I should have just ignored this Irish kid or leveled my usual curse at him, but he surprised me by asking, "What's it worth, mate?"

I stopped and thought for a moment. "I dunno," I said. "Sixty, seventy p, about."

And then he stuffed the bill in his pocket and shuffled off down the street toward Westbourne Grove without a word of thanks or acknowledgment.

I stared after him, transfixed by the sound of the rain spattering on my suitcase. Then I went indoors and made a cup of tea.

# carp fishing
## on valium

"Brian?" said a vaguely familiar voice on the telephone. I was in Kernley, a small suburban village thirty-five miles southwest of London, sitting in my dad's old armchair in the house where I'd grown up. It was twelve-thirty on a sultry July afternoon and I was glued to a women's match from Wimbledon on the television.

"That you, Del?" I inquired, hitting the mute button on the TV's remote.

"None other, none other. Heard you were around, what you up to, then?"

"Oh, not a lot . . . trying to sell the house, y'know, now the folks have passed on. I thought I might be able to hang on to it, do some writing or something, y'know—somewhere quiet."

"Yeah?"

"Yeah, but I think I'll go spare if I hang around here—England drives me barmy."

"You been in the States too long, mate, that's your trouble. Ought to come back more often, you'll be more used to us fuckin' idiots then!"

"I know, I know. Still, not bad right now, is it? Fuckin' hot out there. Funny watching the English deal with the heat."

We had a bit of a laugh at this. Del rarely said anything without a chuckle as punctuation; he was just one of those guys. A real likely lad, he couldn't get through a sentence without cracking up. Del and I had hung out together in our early twenties, pub crawling, smoking dope, and occasionally tempting the odd pair of lifeless, lumpen Surrey girls into the backseats of our secondhand cars.

" 'Ow 'bout comin' fishin', then?" he asked, adding that customary giggle at the end, as if it was a damn funny thing to ask someone you haven't talked to for nigh on seven years.

"Fishing? Been a long time . . ." I said, reluctant to drag myself away from the TV set. "Uh, all right," I finally agreed, remembering Del's persistent nature. "Where?"

"Tomlin's Pond."

Tomlin's Pond: the name rang a bell, but I couldn't remember whether I'd actually fished there or not.

"Where's that at?"

"Borley. Back of the Strauss Estate."

"Fuck me, Del! You mean where all the right fuckin' 'erberts live? Bloody rough 'ouse that estate, in' it?" I asked, my English accent reverting to its old severity with each word exchanged between us.

"Nah, s'all right. I know a few blokes over there. I score dope from Big Den—'e lives there. 'E's all right, s'long as you don't run into 'im when the pubs turn out."

"Dope? You still smokin'?"

"Course. What, you quit? All healthy an' American, are ya?"

"Well, Christ, Del, I am fifty-one, you know. Finally quit cigarettes an' all—still 'ave a drink, though."

"Quit fags? Stroll on! My kidneys are fucked, my chest is wheezin'," said Del proudly, "and I'm stoned most of the day—don't let the bastards grind you down! Know what I mean?"

"Blimey, Del."

Leaving the women tennis players to slog it out on the faded green of Wimbledon's Court Number One, I drove down to Del's parents' old house behind the pub near Borley Green. Typical of Del, he wasn't in, even though I'd just got off the phone with him. So I walked around to the Bag O' Nails, and sure enough, there he was at the bar, king-size Silk Cut in one hand, pint of lager in the other.

"Brian! You look well. John, set Brian up with a pint, will yer?"

"You look well, too, Del. Got a few extra around the gut, though, eh?"

"I know, I gotta get back on the squash court, really, but all the young kids at work are too fuckin' fast for me — they don't give yer a break either, little bastards. 'Ere, get this down yer an' we'll go to Tomlin's."

Although I'd said he looked well, Del had aged a good deal more than I. His face looked puffy and sallow beneath the temporary flush created by the sun. His prominent nose, however, was red and sweaty and had the beginnings of a fine network of drinker's veins. And he was as fat as a pig. Not much hair left either, but his natural ebullience joshed him along and we downed our pints in the empty bar with plenty of laughs.

"This Tomlin's Pond," I wondered out loud, "you say there's carp and tench in there?"

"Yeah, only small ones, like. But we might take a three-pounder. Floatin' crust they go for — the carp, that is. Tench are tiny. Catch 'em for me garden pond."

"What, you own your parents' old house now?" I remembered they had a good-sized concrete pond with frogs and fish in the back garden.

"Yeah, after they died — well, me brother's up north, 'e didn't want it, so I got it. S'handy for work."

"Great, great . . . oh, wait a minute. I remember Tomlin's Pond!"

I'd never actually been to Tomlin's Pond, but I suddenly recalled a long-ago summer when I'd discovered this tempting, unknown body of water in a faded old map that lay sandwiched between a musty stack of *Readers Digests* in the village junk shop. One searing afternoon, I'd met up with Chalkie Wild, a gangly, white-haired kid from down the street, and we stumped off in search of the phantom pond. Although it was supposedly a mere two or three miles from Kernley, nobody—not even the oldest and crustiest fishermen we knew—had heard of the place. That particular summer, Chalkie and I were often out in the still abundant woodlands, hunting down enigmas like Tomlin's Pond—mysterious stuff we'd heard about or seen on maps. One time, our ears picked up the roar of dirt-tracking motorbikes and we dropped whatever we were doing and struck off to find them. Two hours later, we were tightrope-walking the wooden telegraph pole crossbeams of a lock over the Basingstoke Canal near Brookwood, then climbing the fence to the railway tracks before finally giving up. It was getting toward dusk and we were miles from home and no closer to the dirt bikes.

The search for Tomlin's Pond had produced similar results, and after hours of slogging through dense tangles of rhododendrons, brambles, and the occasional back garden, Chalkie and I gave up, unsure of our direction and losing faith in the pond's existence.

"Finish up, then," said Del, chugging back the last of his pint. John, the barman, wiped the bar with an old rag. The room was dense with Del's cigarette smoke, and sunlight carved through the frosted windows, creating beams in the thick blueness.

"Ere, 'ave a blast," said Del, passing me a short, thick joint as we drove through the dozy Sunday-afternoon suburbs toward Tomlin's Pond.

163

"Christ," I groaned. "What are you, Del, forty-seven?"

"Just turned forty-eight," he answered, chuckling through his nose. "Go on!"

"Oh, all right—but the baccy'll probably kill me."

I took a hit and felt the Silk Cut caress my throat and the pungent taste of hashish curl around my tongue.

"They only smoke pure grass in the States," I said, pulling on the joint and getting dizzy. "They never mix it with tobacco."

"I know, I know," giggled Del. "Good, though, in' it?"

"Moroccan?"

"None other, none other."

We arrived at Tomlin's Pond, which was bigger than I'd imagined, kidney-shaped with a small island in the middle. We drove along the road that skirted the whole of one bank. On our right was the notorious Strauss Estate with narrow roads leading into its heart and dotted with small, dull suburban semidetached houses, built in the late sixties. On our left, a yellowing, sun-baked lawn sloped down to the water, but the rest of the pond was flanked by dense bushes and trees. The estate, of course, had not existed in the days when Chalkie and I had had our perigrinations, and probably most of the overgrown route we had pursued would now be similarly overtaken with tarmac, bricks, mortar, and thousands of souls.

Del and I got our gear out and stared across the water, which looked like a tin plate in the hot afternoon sun. A couple of straggly pines grew on the island and a pair of white swans picked around its margins. At the back of the pond, beyond the woods, I could hear the soft drone of traffic from a main road. No one seemed to be about. It was Sunday and the English, already fried from three weeks of high temperature, were indoors digesting their early dinners, watching tennis, or in the pubs.

I followed Del around the back of the pond; there was a small path of black, caked earth that ran between a chain-link fence and the thick foliage that grew on the pond's margins. Not being used to the hash, I felt dwarflike and rubbery as we hustled along the path, beams of sunlight spiking through the tree branches like swords. I felt my tackle box bumping my leg and heard Del's heavy breathing in front of me.

Del had a lolloping, splay-footed gait and bulged out of his clothes: gray, shiny, creased trousers with slight flares at the ankles, a threadbare white shirt that was pointy-collared but, despite its age, newly pressed, and a pair of scuffed black shoes with chunky platform soles. Completing the outfit were two green-and-black-chequered socks so thin I could see gnat bites in the pale flesh beneath the material. He looked like an old guy who had just visited his local Salvation Army store and decked himself out in some youngster's bad disco gear. But I was sure that these were Del's own threads and that he'd owned many an identical outfit since the late seventies.

After what seemed an eternity but could only have been a minute or two, we reached the spot where we would fish, or as English fisherman's vernacular would have it, the swim. The swim was a spit of black, packed-down mud with hawthorns clustering the bank to our left and the chain-link fence behind us following the curve of the pond to our right. There were lily pads growing in the corner, stretching out about fifty feet. Looking left across the pond, I could see Del's car parked on the road and the Strauss Estate beyond it, the houses like small rectangular cakes.

"Looks all right," I said, nodding at the water. "Looks carpy."

"Yeah," agreed Del, "we'll try some floating crust — might tempt somethin' as it cools down a bit."

We set up our rods and threw some pieces of crust to the edge of the lilies, twenty or thirty feet out, hoping to get the carp interested. Per Del's instructions, I threaded a ledger weight onto the six-pound breaking strain line, stopped it with a lead split-shot, and attached a size-twelve hook.

"What's that?" asked Del, looking at my tackle. "Real lead?"

"Yeah."

"Give us a split-shot. Fuckin' great, 'aven't seen real lead for years. I hate this alloy shit — doesn't grip the line well enough, keeps fallin' off. Illegal, y'know — real lead."

"Shows you how long it's been since I went fishing. I've 'ad this for yonks," I said.

Del chuckled. He liked illegal stuff. Anything against the law was all right by him. He was the one who instigated the garden gnome-stealing excursions in the seventies: you'd get a carload of intoxicated guys, drive around the suburbs at three in the morning, and visit the garden gnome territories. Blokes would jump from the car, scale people's gates, grab the gnomes, and throw them into the boot. When a dozen or so had been collected, you'd drive to the edge of town and find a roundabout—preferably one with a little grass and a flower bed on it—and set the gnomes up there. It was a gas if you could swing by at rush hour the next morning and watch people's faces when they drove past on their way to work. Once we stole a boat from someone's front garden and stuck it in the middle of Cronwell High Street. That was a good one, that was.

Del and I cast out and after a few attempts managed to get the baits in position inches from the wall of lily pads. The mechanics of the rigs were simple: the ledgers provided the casting weight to get the bait out there, and the crust, which was lighter than the stop-shot, would float to the surface and tempt the carp. Often the fish felt the line coming up from the bottom and got spooked; but sometimes they'd get so involved with sucking the free samples of bread crust off the surface that one would be tricked into taking a baited hook. Striking and connecting was a different matter—a tricky business really, every bit as skilled as fly-fishing. And then, once hooked, you had to keep the fish out of the lilies.

Del rolled another joint and pulled some Carlsberg Special Brew from his tackle bag. The beer was powerful and warm, quite foul-tasting to me, but English headcases like Del loved it. Then he rummaged through his trouser pockets and pulled out two blue tablets.

" 'Ere, Brian, 'ave a Valium," he said with the customary chuckle.

"Del!"

"Go on, 'ave one. Fifteen milligrams. Swapped 'em for Tuinol."

"You still rippin' off Tuinol from work?"

"Fuckin' right. Good currency, mate, good currency."

Del had worked for Turroughs-Marcon for as long as I had known him, which was about twenty-six years, and regularly stole powerful sleepers like Tuinol, which he liked to mix with drink. Then he'd drive around on the dark country roads after the pubs closed. Once a year, he'd plow into a tree or through someone's front window. But he always came out of it unmarked and, more important, he never seemed to get fined or lose his license or have his nefarious activities discovered: he was just one of those blokes.

I took the Valium, reeled in my line, and rebaited, convinced that the bread, which was difficult to see with the sun beating down on the water, had disintegrated. I cast out again and we sat on our little fold-out plastic chairs and stewed in the sun. The surface of the water was absolutely flat and the whole pond appeared devoid of fish. The traffic, droning hypnotically beyond the trees, the two listless swans cruising the island, and the flies and mosquitoes buzzing around our ears were the only signs of life.

Apart from his floating crust rig, Del had also set up a five-foot fiberglass rod with a small float and a size-sixteen hook baited with a single maggot. He worked this in a dense patch of stringy weed that grew in the corner, adjacent to the lily pads.

In no time the Valium joined the hash and the Special Brew; the three intoxicants buzzed through my bloodstream like an old, untrustworthy friend. I tried staring at the glassy water, hoping to locate my bait, but a rustling in the bushes diverted my attention, and when I turned to look into the leafy depths, lights and stars flashed across my eyes. I returned my gaze to the shallows, black with sediment at the margins, and noticed some tiny insect life darting about. Suddenly a shadow came over me, followed by a roar.

"Jet shuttle to Aussie," said Del, squinting up at the giant craft.

"Did that last year," I said. "Went on a book tour—took two hours, Heathrow to Sydney."

"Shit. What's it like when it leaves the atmosphere?"

"Great. Stars . . . the moon, everything," I answered vaguely. The Valium was really kicking in now and I felt like a rubber band.

We looked up as the rocket arced across the blinding sky. Then I studied my hands and noticed all the veins, as if my skin were transparent. I rubbed my eyes; in the darkness behind the lids, lilies and carp danced around like a Japanese woodcut.

After a few hours, the sinking sun sped up its course near the trees on the far side. The water became blacker and more defined. The skin on its surface broke by the lily pads and something nudged one of the pieces of crust we'd thrown out earlier. I noticed a couple of youths — skinheads by the look of it — messing around on the grassy bank not far from Del's car across the pond. They yelled crudely and threw rocks in the water. The commotion made me nervous.

" 'Ere we go," said Del, suddenly lifting his rod from the ground and striking. The ledger weight flew out of the water and peeled off behind him, hitting the fence with a metallic clank.

"Fuck it, missed," groaned Del, standing up and retrieving his tackle.

"Bite?" I asked, staring hard at where I thought my hook was.

"Think so. Right time for it now."

The float on his other rod began dipping in the weeds and then shot under. Del scrambled for it and struck, this time connecting. He pulled up a tiny dark green tench about three inches long; it flipped around in the air on the silver hook.

"Beautiful!" he exclaimed, unhooking it. Del half-filled a cream-coloured plastic bucket with water and tossed the fish in. Baby tench were a mystery; I'd never seen them before. Usually, you only caught tench when they were about two pounds or more in weight. The adults spawned and the fry just disappeared until they were big; perhaps they hid in the dense weeds or in the mud feeding on microscopic pond life — no one really knew. Del said Tomlin's Pond was the only place he'd ever caught them. I was amazed. I stared into the bucket at the tench and its ruby-red eyes.

Del and I sat down again and squinted at the water. We talked for a while about fishing, work, the current price of dope, the weather—the usual stuff. But we rarely touched on anything serious concerning our personal lives, and when we did, we swiftly brushed over such self-revealing nonsense with Del's trademark chuckle and my general cynicism for all things cozy or open-hearted. French people indulged in maudlin and overly dramatic musings on their lives, and so did Americans. Certainly us English would have no truck with it. So Del and I sat there, quite content in our intoxicated state, chatting meaninglessly, until quite suddenly a tramping sound on the path made us start. There, through the gloaming, came the skinheads I had spotted earlier.

"Fuck me," said one of them as they looked us over. He wore tight, faded Levi's held up by red braces that carved into his bare chest. On his feet were steel toe–capped Doc Martens, and a crude black swastika was tattooed on his forehead. His mate looked identical, except he had a blue knife tattooed on his cheek. Behind them was a third one: short, swarthy, with an ugly unibrow overhanging his piggish eyes. He lurked there in the shadows, blocking the path, and I wondered if more of their mates were about to stomp into view.

Del and I twisted around in our chairs, unsure of how to respond. We were trapped in the corner of the pond, no real way out except for swimming for it.

"You need a fuckin' permit to fish 'ere, cunts!" said the swastika boy with extreme viciousness.

"Nah," said Del lamely.

"Fuck you, granddad. I said, you need a fuckin' permit!"

I started shaking like a leaf.

"Oi, give us a fuckin' Special Brew, you cunt!" snorted the one with the knife tattoo, stomping on the black mud between me and Del as he pulled two cans from the plastic ring holder. The skinheads had tiny, dull eyes that seemed to swallow the light.

"Nice fuckin' rod. I fink I'll 'ave that," said the swastika boy, and he picked up my eleven-foot fibreglass rod and started reeling in the line. The other one said "Duh" as he glugged down some Special Brew. The swarthy boy remained silent, maintaining a remarkably stupid expression. I was fifty-one years old; I couldn't have tackled these lads when I was twenty, let alone now, and this was their specialty—extreme intimidation. But I felt I had to do something. Quietly, I reached my hand out toward my tackle box where I had an old penknife that I'd picked up on the bank of a gravel pit about twenty years ago.

The boy who'd taken my rod suddenly kicked me in the foot; I felt a numb burning masked by the Valium, and drew my hand back quickly, expecting some serious violence.

Then Del spoke: "I know Big Den, pal . . .'e's a mate of mine," he said, his eyes watering and voice quavering. The skins stepped back and thrust out their skinny lips.

"Big Den?" ventured the one with the knife tattoo.

172

"Yeah, fifteen Rosalyn Crescent, on the Strauss Estate. That where you come from, the Strauss?" asked Del, a bit of strength coming back into his voice. "That's where he lives," he continued. "Know his wife Jean, too, and the kids. Big Den is my friend," said Del, standing up.

The skinheads dropped my rod and the Special Brew, and stepped back toward the path.

"All fuckin' right, cunt," sneered the one with the swastika. "So you know Big fuckin' Den, then. Cunts!"

But they'd got the wind up and were clumping back toward the estate.

"Fuckin' bastards, fuckin' bastards!" sang one of them, like a football chant.

I sank back into my chair and reached out for my rod, which lay on the ground between us. Still shaking like a leaf, I let out a huge whistling breath. Del chuckled through his nose.

"Fuckin' idiots . . . you all right?"

"Yeah. I guess so. Jesus, Del, well done, mate."

"No problem, Brian. Legend, Big Den is. You don't fuck with 'im, know what I mean?"

"Whew."


The sun continued its descent and Del pulled out another blue Valium, which we split. I chugged mine back with a can of Special Brew and Del rolled a joint. Now that the sun had lost its intensity, the water by the lily pads came alive and swirls appeared around our floating crusts. I squinted at what I thought was my bait as some thick, yellow lips sucked it from the surface. Sure enough, my line started snaking across the water and I smoothly lifted the rod and struck, connecting with a good, lively weight.

The carp bolted into the stems of the lily pads, but I managed to turn its head and it shot off, confused, into open water. The rod curved in a satisfying arc as I muscled the fish toward the bank and into the waiting landing net. Del lifted him out and laid the net down on the bank. As I unhooked the fish, the rank odour of decaying weed beds and mud filled the air. The carp puffed its thick lips in and out, its barbules dangling like a mandarin's mustache, its bright eye lolling upward.

"Lovely," said Del.

"Beauty," I agreed, releasing the fish. It probably weighed about three pounds.

"Yanks don't fish for carp much, do they?" asked Del.

"Nah . . . some do, but they don't understand 'em. They'd rather hook a half-pound bass that leaps around on the surface than hook something twenty pound that runs like a tank on the bottom. They think they're junk fish — got to be a lot of leapin' around for Americans. Mind you, I've caught carp in Virginia up to fifteen pounds and they don't fight like the ones here do. They're not as smart, either."

"Further from China," said Del with a chuckle.

"Could be," I said. "You gettin' divorced again, Del? Spoke to Jimmy the other day. He said you were."

"Jimmy from Cronwell?"

"Yeah."

"Yeah, second fuckin' marriage . . . life's a bitch, and then you marry one!"

We laughed at this, and then the mosquitoes arrived in droves and the sun finally dipped below the tree line, so we packed up our gear.

Del and I went to the Bag O' Nails for a few pints until I finally felt totally stupefied, and then I drove home.

# tinseltown,

## morocco

t's the Concorde!" gasped Miss Rosenblum, my secretary. "You're on the goddamn Concorde!"

"Oh," I said dully, "you sure?"

"BA 003," she announced dramatically. "Can't be anything else. Leaves New York eight forty-five A.M., arrives Tangier six P.M. I knew there was something weird about that. Lucky bastard! Get your bags packed! Get your passport—Hasimoto is sending a car to pick you up, seven A.M."

Miss Rosenblum was referring to 22nd Century Hasimoto, presently the biggest movie company in Hollywood. Bigger than Sony/Warner. Bigger even than Griffin/Speilbore/Asahi. In the last two years, this upstart organization had amassed millions more than its competitors, much of it on the strength of Frankie Drake's directorial savvy. His blockbusters, *Home and Away, Home and Away 2,* and *Mrs. Gunshot,* alone had pushed 22nd Century into the box office stratosphere. They wanted to fly me to Tangier at a moment's notice to sing on a tune slated for the soundtrack of Drake's impending megahit, *9½ Months,* starring Hugh Cry, the latest in a long line of pretty-boy Englishmen who had been scrambling the hormones of American females for much of the late nineties.

I looked around the tiny dressing room of the Corpuscle Club in Manhattan while Miss Rosenblum excitedly detailed this hastily conceived engagement in her colourful Queens accent.

"Let me get this straight, Miss Rosenblum," I said, wiping the post-gig perspiration from my forehead and staring distractedly at the pay phone dial. I'd just played to a minute audience in a room that only held 150 people, on a Friday night at that. There couldn't have been more than fifty out there. Only a year ago I'd packed the place with the same exciting lineup: me on guitars, mouth organ, and vocals; George Weidy, a one-toothed bass player I'd picked up in the Appalachians in '98; and Bracknia, a plump girl with a lot of face furniture in the form of studs, rings, and crucifixes, all pierced neatly through the place where her eyebrows used to be like curtains in a Bangkok knockin' shop. Formidable a sight as Bracknia was, she could play percussion instruments with an endearing earnestness and had thrown herself into my material, though I suspected Ketamine Techno was more her thing. She was the only percussionist I'd ever seen who had put the flat of her hand clean through a Nigerian goatskin bongo — like it was cardboard! An incredible achievement, really, and the talk of the circuit for months after.

The moment our set had finished, George and Bracknia stepped off the stage and went straight to the bar, probably to try and scare up some women. But I skulked off alone to the coffinlike dressing room, embarrassed by the size of the crowd and worn out from constant gigging for zero reward. And besides, I had to get on the phone ASAP to talk to Miss Rosenblum and see if this soundtrack bullshit was really on.

". . . Let me get this straight. They are flying me to Tangier, Morocco, on the Concorde, tomorrow morning, to do one vocal on this Small Billy song" — here, I tapped the cassette of the alleged piece of music on the wall of the dressing room, right between the loins of a cartoon female with a vagina like the Mersey Tunnel — "and they're putting me up in the best hotel and paying me ten grand — just for starters?"

"You got it," came the nasal Queens response. "Then God knows what residuals and lucrative guest appearances you could be gettin' outta this . . . you're not considering not doing it, are ya?"

"If you insist, Miss Rosenblum. God, you're a slave driver!"

"You lucky bastard! The Concorde!"

---

As a persistent September drizzle filled the New York sky, I boarded the glistening supersonic jet bang-on at 8:15 A.M., earning a few arched eyebrows from the brushed-suede-and-cashmere set due to my funky garb: yellow steel toe–capped work boots, black, ill-fitting Jet Heavy jeans, and a multihued, squiggly-patterned shirt with a collar long since threadbare. Even the Concorde, with its downturned nose, appeared—at least to my slushy, hungover eye—to regard me with haughtiness. Once in my seat, I appraised the leather folder in the seat pocket in front of me with a forced casualness, dying to get my hands on it and rip off the shrink wrap to winkle out the free goodies inside. But I mustered enough restraint to resist a plunder until we were well on our way, noting the Concorde clientele's complete disinterest in the freebies.

The clean and coiffured passengers had more important affairs to deal with. Within minutes of takeoff, a flurry of laptops flipped open, sporting brilliant full-colour graphics, dense accounts of multi-zeroed figures, intricate architectural designs, and a plethora of other high-powered business motifs. I felt like I was in a flying bank or some space module peopled with dignitaries whose careening, mouse-moving fingers controlled the very pulse of the global economy.

Caviar, game pie, and champagne appeared in great quantities. After a few brimming glasses, my cool broke completely: I lunged at the soft grey leather pouch in the seat pocket and tore into its shrink wrap with my teeth. Inside the pouch was a glossy pamphlet detailing the history of supersonic travel, some postcards of the Concorde in various semi-erotic positions, and a sleek silver pen engraved with the vessel's insignia that was snuggled in a soft felt jacket of slate grey.

Ah, this was the way to go! A warm glow spread over my body as I signaled the svelte air hostess for more champagne, and repeatedly clicked the cool silver pen in my right ear. The sound of the ballpoint, constantly disappearing and re-emerging with its couched, dulcet tones made me drowsy, and I nodded for a while in a sea of soft clicks.

I awoke with a start as we hit Mach 2, somewhere over the Atlantic Ocean, 53,000 feet below. I had homework to do. I needed to listen to Small Billy's song to get the feel of the arrangement. Although the tune was merely a Stones ballad-by-the-numbers, I wanted that sucker firmly in my head.

Chorus, verse, chorus, verse, chorus, solo modulation, verse, chorus; slow Keith Richards B-side in G major — piece of cake. I'd knock the thing out in an hour and bugger off to the medina, pick up a caftan, and sit in the sun with a kif pipe for the rest of the day. The contrast between last night at the Corpuscle Club and this morning with the Concorde Club, heading to an easy singing gig and a few days in the Rashid Hotel, Tangier's finest, was infinitely delicious and pleasantly heightened by the waft of expensive perfumes and delicate aftershaves.

I thanked God for the fact that Small Billy, a fine guitarist, peripheral journeyman, and sometime accomplice of the superstar Speigelstein, was a lousy singer. His vocal on the tape was, in fact, a wince-inducing racket of overly mannered Stonesism, clichéd to high heaven and riddled with would-be emotion. I thanked God that Frankie Drake had sat down with Small Billy, and that the two of them had come up with my name as the man for the job. They'd given 22nd Century Hasimoto the green light to rush me out—no expense spared—to Tangier.

I thanked God (or, as my thoughts turned to caftans and kif, Mohammed) for the superstar rock band Bonhomie, and Ron Bonhomie himself, the leader, who had invited Small Billy out on his world tour as second guitarist and general groove merchant, in support of Bonhomie's new megaplatinum LP, whose title was so bland I could never remember it, just like the grandiloquent, over-reaching songs it contained. I thanked God most of all for the fact that Bonhomie and Small Billy were in Tangier, for it meant I could lie around for a few days drinking mint tea, eating couscous, and getting stoned—and then stick the bill to 22nd Century Hasimoto! Not one thin dirham would I be spending on this one—not on your life!

As the clean-skinned, velvety passengers of the Concorde prepared to disembark at Tangier International, I noticed a good many dipping surreptitiously into their seat pockets to pull out the leather folders, as if in afterthought, as if it mattered not a whit whether they collected their free gifts or left them to the cleaners. It brought the whole gaggle of them down to more basic, human terms. Despite the brief duration of the flight, I did perceive a few rumpled collars, a few hairs out of place, and one or two scuffs on shoes and computers.

"That was quick," I said to the small Japanese gentleman in the seat next to me as we rose to leave.

"Quick," he agreed, keeping a distance from my ripped plastic shoulder bag and gardening boots.

Once past immigration, which was agreeably nonconfrontational due to our prestigious mode of transport, I was greeted by Hussien, a runner sent out by Bonhomie's tour manager, in a black-windowed limo. We whisked through the stone streets and casbahs of Tangier to the luxurious Rashid Hotel. A room key was handed to me immediately upon entering the cool white marble reception area. My high-ceilinged suite overlooked a shady inner courtyard. I immediately called room service and ordered several lentil dishes with couscous and a glass pitcher of sweet mint tea. After the meal, I lay on the bed and drowsily stared at the broad, slow paddles of the ceiling fan until the phone rang, and Small Billy's New Jersey drawl sounded in my ear.

"BP, you made it, man!"

"Hey, Small Billy. How the devil are you, pal, all right? It's been years."

"Man, it's been a while. Great to have you on this thing. Listen: we couldn't get the studio for tomorrow, so you got a day to hang, all right?"

"No problem, what happened?" Here we go, I thought: the complications had begun already.

"Well, there's some fuckin' band in there that I thought we could bump. But they won't move. They're out tomorrow night, no question. We gotta get this done, the movie's out in two months. Wanna drink? Down at the bar in ten?"

"Be there, Billy."

"See ya."

In the bar, the early-evening sunlight played through the windows on the blue-and-white-tiled interior. Small Billy, Irish coffee in hand, leapt up from a shady sofa and embraced me fondly.

"Hey, man, long time!"

"Long time? Jesus, it's been what . . . eighteen years?" I queried.

"Eighteen? Must be, must be," agreed Billy, scratching his jaw and clicking his fingers at the bartender. "Ali, get this man a drink. Wadda ya want, BP?"

I ordered a Singapore Sling and sat down on the white linen sofa, eyeing Small Billy, marveling that a guy his age was still playing the renegade rock 'n' roller for all it's worth. The broad paisley bandanna around what I presumed was a bald head was so tight and impermeable, it looked as if it grew there, like a skin extension. A baggy white silk shirt flowed around his chest, reminding me of one of the stoned-out dancing Beatles' wives or girlfriends in the "All You Need Is Love" clip from the sixties. Billy's pants were black and floppy at the waist, but tight at the ankles, and on his feet were a pair of black, soft leather moccasins. Alarmingly, he wore no socks.

We chatted for a while about the old days, when we had co-headlined a tour together. Our recollections, with the distance of time, seemed rosy, idyllic. But as we en-thused about various touring shenanigans, often guffawing at the memory of this or that hilarious incident, images of Billy acting the pop star prima donna and being a giant pain in the butt came back to me. The guy was a good guitarist, no question. But he did ponce around a bit, like he thought he was much more. I found myself hoping that this engagement would be as simple as it appeared, and that Small Billy's ego would not puff up like his billowing white shirt.

His cellular phone rang suddenly. Billy launched into a difficult conversation with someone named Mohammed, who evidently ran the studio where we were booked to do the vocal.

". . . Okay, okay," said Billy, giving me a wink and roll-ing his eyes. "Okay, Mohammed, listen. Amplifiers. You know? Amplifiers? Er . . . they're the things that you plug guitars into that make the sound. Shit, what's Moroccan for amplifiers? Amplifiers, yeah. You know: Marshals, Fenders, all that stuff. A fez? What the fuck's a fez? Is it an amp? Okay, Okay. Look, we'll take it, all right? Yeah, yeah . . . as many amplifiers and fezzes as you can get. No, no . . . you're not understanding me, Mohammed. 22nd Century Hasimoto are paying for *everything*. Everything, okay? Everything. The food, the dope, the belly dancers. Whatever the fuck it is, 22nd Century is paying. Right. Good. Talk to you later, bye."

"He didn't know the word 'amplifiers'?" I asked incred-ulously.

"He didn't know shit. Biggest studio in Morocco and he didn't know what an amp is. Fuck."

"Are you doing some overdubs on this thing, Billy?"

"Yeah. It's just a basic that you heard. I got some of the Bonhomies coming in after you. Replace the bass, a little piano, Dickie Sambucca's gonna play a little slide."

*Ouch,* I thought. The backing track already sounded overloaded, what with the mandolins and accordions and all the rest of it chiseling away.

"Gonna have to go forty-eight track?" I asked, pretending to know what I was talking about.

"Yeah," agreed Billy, "they're flying another machine in from Paris or somewhere. You know, I just wanna improve it a little. Just a few nice touches."

"Great," I said, stabbing myself in the eyeball with a paper umbrella as I gulped the Singapore Sling. "Funny," I said, "I always get a pain in the right eye when I drink Singapore Slings."

Billy roared with laughter. "Same as ever, eh, BP? Sense of humour intact!"

"Eh, Billy," I said, feigning a serious look.

"What?"

"Know where I can score some dope in this town?"

"Ahhh ha ha ha ha ha! Very funny, man. Very funny!"


I left Small Billy to further intricate telephone conundrums with the locals and sloped off outside. Warm Moroccan twilight dappled the red sandstone streets. My peregrina-

tions brought me to the medina, where I soon attracted—
as I browsed the basket weaving stalls—a small coterie of
scruffy kids and mutilated beggars who called me "Jimi"
or "John" or "Hey, Mr. Beatle!" One little devil was particularly insistent upon prizing a few dirhams from my
pocket. He followed me for ten minutes, all the while in-
sisting that I was "Hey, Michael Jackson!" Eventually,
when I thought no one was looking, I cuffed the beggar
around the ear and he ran off, muttering guttural Arabic
curses, his rags flapping around his dirty knees.

Back on the streets, I found a small non-tourist cafe
and sat in the corner with a mint tea. In the opposite corner of the room, not five feet away, a cluster of men
smoked kif and watched a Godzilla movie on a black-and-
white TV, laughing quietly at the monster's antics. The
smell of kif was tempting and before long I had caught the
eye of a short, hawk-nosed man who shuffled over from
the group and offered me a pipe. I sucked on the clay
contraption and handed it back, nodding affirmatively.
Gradually, the tiled walls took on a soft liquidity and Majeed's face (he had, at some point, introduced himself) rippled with the desert mystery of the Bedouins in the glow
of the candle at our table.

"It good," he said, infinitely slowly, "for the med."

As Majeed spoke he pointed to his head, which was
covered by the hood of his djellaba.

"Meditation?" I queried. "Yes, it is good for meditation," I agreed, a stupid grin creeping across my face.

"Good," he repeated slowly, "for the *med.*"

187

"Ah," I said, twigging it. "You mean the *head.*"

"Ah yes!" he exclaimed. "Good for *head!*"

"Right, man!"

Majeed produced a small folded packet of kif; I handed him twenty dirhams and left, thoroughly stoned. Back in the medina, I bought a clay pipe and returned to the hotel, where I ran into the namesake of the supergroup himself, Ron Bonhomie.

He invited me to his table in the courtyard. We sat in the flicker of soft candlelight as the thin branches of lemon trees, melodious with crickets and tree frogs, stroked across the black, starry sky above us. I ordered another Singapore Sling and Ron drank a Coke. Two burly minders flanked us, sipping mint tea and anxiously fingering a variety of pagers, walkie-talkies, and pencil phones.

"Good to have you on this thing, man," said Ron, imperious behind his impossible good looks, perfect teeth, and black Ray-Bans.

What the hell did he have to do with it? I thought. Is he singing on the track, too? Did someone neglect to tell me a duet was on the cards? Thinking about the song, I suddenly wondered why I'd been chosen anyway; to my mind, Small Billy's guide vocal suggested a style closer to Bonhomie's than mine, with its excessive angst lending itself to the "all-mouth-and-trousers" technique.

"Yeah . . . man," I agreed lamely, still unable to wipe the idiotic grin off my face, which I'd sported since that first pipe of kif an eternity ago.

Ron crapped on incomprehensibly about platinum record parties, outselling his competitors (he bandied some hefty names about here), and plenty of other big-time stuff that I found exceedingly dull. Becoming bored, I pulled out my new clay pipe and began to fill it with kif.

"No," insisted one of Ron's minders flatly.

"Not around Ron, please, Brian," asserted the other.

"Ah . . ."

"Sorry, man," said Ron, suddenly looking very uncomfortable, "but anything like that and its 'Bonhomie Dope-Smoking Wild Orgies!' in the tabloids in the States by tomorrow morning."

"Shit, what a drag. It's more or less legal here, isn't it?"

"Don't matter, man. Don't matter." He eyed the lemon trees, presumably scouting for paparazzi hanging from the boughs.

"I can dig it," I said, and put the gear away. I was the one who was stoned, but he was the one who was paranoid. I ordered another Sling and we fell into silence.

After a while one of the Bonhomie band members arrived and sat next to Ron. As they bantered with in-joke on-the-road camaraderie, I spaced out a little, mesmerized by the sounds of cutlery clinking in the courtyard, mosquitoes reconnoitering in my ears, muffled, respectful conversation between the waiters, and the distant drone of pipes and percussion from beyond the walls, out in the thick Moroccan night. I would rest up tomorrow, wander around the medina, cuff a few young beggars, smoke a little kif, and order as many expensive items on room service as I could. Ah, this was really living!

Indeed, on my day off I rested well, but the morning after eventually arrived. I stepped from the marble hotel reception and into a waiting limo-van, which crawled through the narrow Tangier streets toward Mohammed Sound, Morocco's finest studio. My driver, a young, overeager chap named Mukraik, pointed out the bargain brothels and kif-purchasing cafes along the way, but I paid little attention. My mind was on Small Billy's song, analyzing its structure and the various attack modes my vocal would assume for each piece of the jigsaw.

There was nothing complex about the number, which was entitled "Their Life and Their Times." Still, I had this nagging feeling. It had reared up on my first meeting with Ron Bonhomie and I couldn't seem to shake it. Surely, I thought, if Ron himself was here in Morocco, with the day off (before the whole entourage was shipped off to Rabat for a two-night stand at the Capital Bigdome), why didn't anyone think of him as guest vocalist? Why me? Sure, for a few aging hepcats I would be the infinitely cooler choice, and the reality of my style knocked Ron and his ilk into a cocked hat. But if he did the song, there was every chance it would become a huge hit. Ron Bonhomie's aching hysterics would nail that sucker right into the hearts of the preteen, moon-eyed millions who lapped up sanitized pop like cotton candy.

Brittle slashes of sunlight scythed between the red sandstone buildings as the limo crawled toward the studio, but with every flicker of light my sense of gloom mysteriously deepened.

Eventually Mukraik brought the vehicle to a halt by a pair of giant leather doors in a narrow alleyway. He indicated that this was in fact the studio entrance and not some private belly dancing club, which I had assumed to be the case. Why *not* me? I assured myself as the hefty portals swung open and a sloe-eyed boy in a clean white djellaba beckoned me in. Frankie Drake wanted me. The movie was a romantic comedy featuring a young couple and an overlong pregnancy; it was not some trashy effects-driven roller coaster designed for short-attention-spanned youth. It was a film for adults and Frankie needed an adult, soulful vocal, suitable for a probing, adult song, and not some phony hormonal "rock" histrionics. That was it, pure and simple. He and Billy fancied me for the job and 22nd Century Hasimoto had flown me over at great expense to do it. And do it I would. Damn these negative emotions! It was just nerves. Always, in this game, there are nerves.

As I walked into the studio's control room, I was immediately struck by the sheer antiseptics of the joint. The place was utterly vibeless, and I felt that I was about to have a lung removed or some similar medical procedure, rather than submit an emotive vocal performance.

The carpet under my feet reminded me of the drab beige cut of material you might find in an English suburban insurance office. The paneled walls sported slats of cheap Formica-like wood, probably reconstituted pine mulch from Scandinavia. But what really grabbed my attention was the console. It was a gothic monstrosity, totally incongruous with its sterile surroundings. Small Billy, his googly eyes scanning the controls, looked ready to take a hammer to this device, which was, judging from the intense hieroglyphics scrawled across its controls, of a most peculiar Arabic design.

"Can you dig this thing, BP?" said an exasperated Billy.

"Wow," was all I could muster.

"Wow is right, man. What a fuckin' doozy this baby is!"

Sitting next to Billy was a middle-aged Moroccan in a cheap blue suit and white shirt with sandals on his bare feet. He introduced himself to me without much enthusiasm as Abdullah, the studio's resident engineer.

"It is an Akmed Majeer," he explained. "Moroccan design—very nice."

"Yeah, yeah, Abdullah," said Billy, his eyes bulging out in his round baby face. "An Akmed Majeer, great. How the fuck do you work the thing?"

"The red knob is volume," said Abdullah, pointing to an enormous dial at Billy's left elbow, as if that explained everything.

I craned over Billy's shoulder, marveling at the intricate, bejeweled faders and buttons, the Arabic symbols and hand-carved wooden pan pots, and the sheer density of EQ switches and beaded coloured lights that glimmered between them. The whole ornate creation was like a half-forgotten, kif-induced dream.

"This sucker?" asked a sweating Billy, pointing at the massive dial.

"Volume," insisted Abdullah, nodding with languid eyes, like he was examining a belly dancer's groin.

Billy finally got the track up on the speakers, which were, thankfully, a hefty pair of German 832s. I winced as Billy's cracked, croaking vocal cut through the maze of acoustic guitars, accordions, and synthesized string parts. Again, I felt a sense of grim foreboding in my gut; Billy's delivery sure as hell sounded like a poor man's Bonhomie. But I steeled myself, walked casually into the vocal booth, and donned a pair of earphones.

Billy's disembodied voice crackled in the cans, instructing me to try a variety of microphones, two of them Arabic jobs. When he seemed satisfied that he had found a mike that suited my voice, he ran the track and I began singing, feeling my way into the piece.

The first thing I noticed was how slow the song felt in the cold reality of the recording studio. It appeared leaden, as if it were playing at the wrong speed.

"Go back to the top, will you," I ordered, having become lost somewhere around the second bridge. I had to repace myself here; cassettes and Walkmans nearly always run fast and actual tempos are often a shock. No problem, I told myself. Relax, feel your way into it. Just sing slower! Come on now, BP, you can knock this out in an hour. Piece of cake, remember?

And so, with a few deep breaths on the countoff, I laid

into the song. Within three and a half minutes I had what I thought was a fair first take. I considered asking Billy if he thought any of it might be usable, as I am a great believer in spontaneity. But when I saw the look on Small Billy's face through the glass of the vocal booth, I felt those twinges of doom returning; that lightheaded, sweaty feeling of doubt that every artist must regularly face washed over me. Small Billy, his beringed hand lightly touching the paisley bandanna on his head, his big googly eyes staring distractedly at the Akmed Majeer, sported a hangdog expression that urged me to quickly demand that he reel back the tape.

"Okay, from the top again, Billy. Just getting into it," I said, marshaling a semblance of authority and control, as if my first attempt were merely a rough map for the brilliance that was yet to come. But in my heart, I thought my first attempt had been pretty damn good.

"Yeah, Brian . . . there's a few, you know . . . a few bits of the melody you gotta get which are kind of, you know . . . important. Just, ah . . . just give it another go. You'll get there," urged Billy.

I had been hoping for a more positive reaction, it is truthful to say. But I said to myself that that was silly of me: how many vocalists nail a strange song they didn't write in one take? Well, me for one, I thought, remembering the gleeful reaction of most producers when they hear my voice on a guest vocal spot, a backing vocal, or a tribute album appearance. Shit! What did he mean, "a few bits of the melody . . . which are kind of . . . important"? Melody? It wasn't exactly "Let It Be" he'd written here.

The hi-hat countoff clicked again like an insect in my ear. I lunged into the tune, this time with more gusto, more overtly dramatic delivery. But still, after the last chorus repeats had been completed and the tape stopped and began to rewind, there was an ominous silence from the control booth. I glugged at my bottled water and threw a surreptitious glance at Billy, whose expression had not changed.

"Um . . . getting anywhere?" I hazarded.

"Yeah, yeah. Ah . . . you know, there's just a few things . . . it's a, you know, a funny little song. There's just a few little things in the melody which are kind of . . . important. You know?"

No, I did not know.

"Okay, like what?" I asked, slipping the cans from my head and joining Billy at the board, where he sat fiddling distractedly with the incomprehensible buttons and faders, a decidedly non-groovy hunch gripping his shoulders.

"Well, like every time you sing the last words on the bridges, it should be like 'paaaast' and 'laaaast,' know what I'm saying?"

"Right."

"And on the word 'time,' it should be 'ti-ii-ime.' You know, stuff like that."

"Right, okay. Let me hear your vocal again."

Tiny beads of sweat appeared in the roots of my hair. Something bubbled under my skin, percolating ominously.

I listened in disbelief to his guide vocal. Did he actually want me to perform, note for note, his dated, clichéd Jaggerisms, like it was 1971 or something?

The bubbling under my skin worked its way up to my jaw and into my fingers; they began to flex automatically as I leaned over Small Billy, who remained hunched in the swivel chair. I didn't know it quite then, but perhaps if I had recognized my true feelings and said something, instead of quietly listening to his ludicrous suggestions concerning trite vocal gymnastics and "important" melodic turns, I could have avoided what came next.

Instead I merely nodded, muttered something about how doing other people's songs was a little strange for me, and headed back into the vocal booth for another go. I glanced through the glass on the countoff and noticed Billy leaning over to Abdullah the engineer and saying something sharp to him.

I launched into the song again, this time copying plenty of Small Billy's arch phrasing. But halfway through the take I noticed that he was not even at the console, that he had left the room (perhaps even the building!). Only Abdullah remained, glum and swarthy and totally disinterested, uncomprehending of the whole shebang.

After the take, I strolled casually back into the control room, just as Billy entered with three members of the Bonhomie band: Pips, the keyboard player, Rikki Tikki Greenblatt, the percussionist, and Dickie Sambucca, the leather-trousered black-haired guitar wizard, looking for all the world like he had just strolled out of a bad mid-eighties "hard rock" video. I instantly disliked them, despite their mechanical enthusiasm for my vocal take, which now blasted through the speakers.

Billy listened to the performance with deadly serious-ness and pointed out the "important" parts of the "melody" that I was apparently still somehow "not quite getting." I felt embarrassed in front of the band members, who, to my way of thinking, seemed all too cheerful and blemish-free to be real rock 'n' rollers. They just didn't have that intan-gible attitude that is somehow engraved upon the soul of the Real Thing. I knew then, with utmost clarity, why I worked with the emotional cripples who had, over the years, been members of my ever-changing backup band: *they* were the Real Thing, not like these plasticheads who paraded before me now.

Suddenly, halfway through yet another vocal take, Small Billy stopped the tape. He announced quietly that he thought we'd nailed it and that he did not want to be in the studio until four A.M. "Lets get on with the over-dubs!" he roared impatiently. And so Pips, the keyboard player, sauntered into the clinical confines of the recording room and began gracing the piano with some technically perfect but emotionally empty boogie-woogie piano warm-ups.

I sat numb in a swivel chair and watched the overdub scenario unfold before me as if behind glass, as if my mind was locked in its own vocal booth, cut off from real-time events. Every time the track played, I noticed an almost imperceptible cringe ripple across Small Billy's face; often, he would leap up and leave the room and enter a small annex where a telephone sat amongst banks of machinery. I was sure that he was calling Frankie Drake and expressing his doubts about my performance. Occasionally, Billy would stroll off with one of the musicians, sometimes all of them, only to reenter the control room minutes later, looking like nothing was going on. But I was convinced that he had been congealing with them in a most viscous, buddy-buddy, arm-over-the-shoulder manner, expressing his doubts, maintaining that in fact his vocal was more suitable for the job than mine, and that this whole idea was a mistake.

As the warm Moroccan dusk settled on the streets outside and Rikki Tikki laid down some unnecessary percussive elements, this suspicion—nay, certainty—of artistic conspiracy brewed to a boil until finally I could take it no more. Casually drifting from the chair I had been nailed to for hours, I floated over to Small Billy and the Akmed Majeer. I leaned over Small Billy, who now appeared doll-like and doughy.

"That first chorus, I think it's slightly out of pitch. Shall I try it again?" I said robotically.

Small Billy did not look into my eyes; instead he threw a small, doubtful glance at my midriff. "No . . . no, I think it's all right," he said, without a trace of enthusiasm. But I knew it was not all right. I also knew that Small Billy had no intention of using my vocal, therefore he had no intention of correcting it. Suddenly I found my fingers were around his thick neck and I was squeezing with all my might. . . .


For one brief hour, the Moroccan sun, as it sinks slowly in the west, breaks through the tiny slat that serves as my window, and I crane my fevered brow up toward its red light. There must be buildings behind my cell, for at certain times of the day, I hear the distant clanking of metal— perhaps kitchen utensils—and the blurred voices of Arabs. Perhaps if there were no such buildings I would get more sunlight than that one brief hour. I calculate it to be an hour, but in truth, it is only guesswork, for most of my time is spent in a grim half-light that plunges, shortly after the sun has set, into complete blackness. I am at my most desperate and disconsolate then, and cannot escape the constant reliving of the offense, the endless slo-mo replays that serve as my internal cinema during my interminable stay here in Rabat Prison.

I visited Rabat, Morocco's capital, some thirty years ago whilst traveling the hippie trail and found it cold and remote compared with the other cities, and not worth staying in for more than a day. Droves of freaks ferried from Málaga on the southern tip of Spain, across the Strait of Gibraltar to Tétouan, west to Tangier, south to Fez and Meknès; a brief stopover in Rabat, then south to Casablanca and Marrakech. The more adventurous, myself included, might end up in less discovered gems like the lovely seaside town of Essaouira on the fair southwest coast.

But try as I may, I cannot effectively recall the details of those distant times in these early days of prison life. I have to be content with the vivid reenactment of the crime that has put me behind bars, the crime that will be my undoing for a very long time.

It was not my fingers around Small Billy's stout neck that landed me here. That action, heinous as it was, might simply have resulted in an irksome lawsuit from the poor, winded chap and surely no severe repercussions would have ensued. No, what happened after the Bonhomie band members had pried my steely fingers from a red-faced, choking Billy is what put me behind bars, mere feet away from lunatics and sodomites of every stripe. For when they managed to free him from my powerful grip and he had fallen coughing and prostrate onto that cheap, static-laden beige studio carpet, I committed the real crime. The crime I would live to regret for perhaps the rest of my days.

A paring knife rested on the console, its blade glinting in the light of those ornate, false-ruby encrusted switches. I lunged at it, and Abdullah the engineer (who not moments before had been using the knife to casually peel a pomegranate) bolted from his languorous demeanor and threw himself upon me. The five-inch blade sliced diagonally through his jugular, the bone handle still in the grip of my wicked, locked fingers. Abdullah stared at me for a moment as the blood spat out of him onto the Akmed

Majeer, running in rivulets down the slots of the console's faders. In my anger, my grip did not budge, and as Abdullah slid earthwards, the sharp knife opened his neck like a slaughtered pig.

When the police arrived, they found a small packet of kif in my pocket, which did not help matters. Kif is marijuana chopped fine and mixed with equally finely chopped tobacco; strangely enough, it's the tobacco that is illegal. The tobacco is grown clandestinely in the valleys west of the Atlas Mountains and therefore untaxed. The labyrinthine Moroccan laws maintain that possession of this tobacco is a crime worthy of lengthy prison sentences—at least if the authorities wish to make an example of a foreigner. Unfortunately, possessing that small quantity was enough, to the Arab legal mind, to illustrate my inherent criminality and push my sentence away from the realms of accident and firmly into one of irredeemable murder. In short order, I found myself in a cavernous, echoing courtroom, facing a gnomelike French/Moroccan judge, whose hatred for good-for-nothing English pop singers was all too evident.

The trial was as Kafkaesque as one might expect and I was not allowed a Western lawyer. I had to settle for a corpulent, one-armed Arab devil, who looked upon me with disdain from the get-go. And that is how I find myself in Rabat Prison, scratching notes on the sticky walls of my tiny cell, recording the recent events with a thin pebble serving as pencil—the only object, apart from the filthy chamberpot, sharing time with me. And once, entwined within the muted sounds of the prison kitchen, I swear I heard a snatch of Small Billy's song, "Their Life and Their Times," on a radio, and with it the pompous bellow of Ron Bonhomie's voice.

I have not, as yet, been sodomized by the inmates, but they will surely get around to that when I am released from solitary. Buulfar, my warden, would love to do the deed, but fortunately for me, the poor blubbery imbecile is a eunuch and can only beat me savagely when the mood takes him. The balls of my feet have already been clubbed by the prison governor, a thin sadist with a Hitler mustache. Many days later (how many? how long have I been here, cramped in the dark?), they are still swollen and incredibly painful.

Occasionally, the eunuch warden squeals at me from outside the cell door in his high, birdlike voice to keep the noise down. And I stop ranting, unaware until then that I was uttering a sound. But I realize soon enough that I have been cursing Small Billy, screaming at his insolence, his nerve to hire me as a vocalist and expect me not to interpret his half-assed tune, but to actually impersonate him *cliché intacto*, as if I had been hired to perform a jingle, as if I were some hack double-scale session man. And I try to conjure up those halcyon memories of my youthful adventures in Morocco, before I became a professional musician, before the Small Billys of the world came sailing in. But my mind cannot step off its angry treadmill. Perhaps later the memories will come back—after all, I have a lot of time.

# the birdman
# of cleveland

So you've got the pilgrims, all duded up with the big hats and shit, on the *Mayflower,* all classes of vomit from seasickness crusting their Van Dykes, every time one of them raises an arm the pong that comes from his armpit'll knock a hog on its ass, and they land on Plymouth Rock all ready to move in, like they own the place or something—" (*mild titters from the audience, although some are still shifting uncomfortably from the crack about how L.A. would become totally dysfunctional if all the illegal Mexicans were kicked out*) "—and there's Tonto and Running Bear and Big Chief Ingrowing Toenail—" (*here, a nice warm wave of reasonable mirth, which I raise my eyebrows at and milk for three or four more seconds*) "—and even though, EVEN THOUGH!—" (*I practically bellow this Eric Morecombe–style and, again, the warm wave is attenuated brilliantly by a Moe-like widening of the eye-balls from Yours Truly*) "—even though these dumbass Indians—Native Americans! Sorry! These, ahem, Native Americans—" (*titters*) "—don't know shit from shoelaces when it comes to the advanced technologies of the white man; even though this powwow of featherheads wouldn't know a combustion engine from a spinning Jenny . . . the bastards really have—" (*each word emphasized slowly and deliberately here as I go for the punch line*) "—THEIR IMMIGRATION SHIT TOGETHER!!" (*A real roar from the fifty or so people and I know I'm on a winner if I can just keep on the ball and not get distracted by the blue-rinsed pair now arriving at the back of the club or the sheer volume of silicone that moves unnaturally under the satin dresses every time a laugh erupts in those Californian chests.*) " 'Where you from?'—" (*Somehow, regardless of the fact that it's my first attempt at this dangerous sketch, which I basically wrote on the flight from Frisco to LAX at one o'clock this morning, I've managed to assume a fair Indian—whoops! Native American—accent, and the punt-ers chuckle happily along, interrupting my flow in the best possible way, so that I have to pause before punch lines and use the spaces, continually emitting nuanced body lan-guage, expertly milking that extra laugh from the Big Laugher at the back, the one that every comedian loves, because when the guy continues to laugh in almost-but-not-quite gut-wrenching convulsions after everyone else's tittcrs have all but decayed, one timely eyebrow raise from Yours Truly will get 'em rolling again and their funny bones'll be well oiled for a big roar of applause and approval at the end of the set, which is coming, as they know, as they can feel.)* " 'Where you from?' says Big Chief Lightinthefuckinhead." *(Big roars at this!)* " 'I . . . I . . . I . . . ' stammers Samuel B. Crumpet, spokesperson-in-a-stovepipe for the whiteass bastards from England who want every fuckin' thing that crosses their fuckin' transoms." *(Nice chuckles here.)* " 'Which land?' asks the chief, stony-faced, arms across chest, part of his right hand resting on a tommyhawk. " 'England?' stammers a confused Samuel B." *(Stcady giggles: they're still with me.)* "Big Chief Lightinthefuckinhead nods to some officious-looking squaw who pulls out a form and asks for Sammy's particulars and his passport. 'No passport?' asks the chief incredulously. 'Give him temporary. Stamp for one week,' he tells the squaw, who pulls out a fucking HUGE rubber stamp and whacks the sucker down on the form." *(The punters are now officially splitting their aerobicized sides. Yessss.)* "Whoops," *(I say, glancing at my watch)* "it's been well over a week, folks, our ship leaves in ten. C'mon, off your asses! This ain't your fuckin' country! Get outta here!! Thank you! Thank you! Take it easy! See ya soon!"

*(And I'm off the stage to a rousing ovation and the MC's got the mike and he's bellowing, "Ladies and Gennelmen . . . nice to have him back at the Comedy Store . . . Brian Porker!!!" and I leap back out for a final bow and that's California behind me and none too shabby, I'd say.)*

"Beautiful! Beautiful! That Indian—"

"Native American," I correct.

"—Native American gag is classy shit, BP! You had 'em rollin' in the fuckin' aisles!" enthuses my agent, Perry Shmucker. "Pure tootski, BP. Wired the fuckers up. Gee, I'd hate to be Artie right now."

We peek through the faded blue velvet curtain at Artie Caseload, who is already onstage, going through the long, slow wind-up of his act, which is a Steven Wrightesque Catatonic-on-Prozac type thing sure to make the crowd fidget after my transatlantic amphetamine approach.

"Ah, he'll get 'em," I reckon. "They're a pushover, this crowd—for L.A."

"Yeah, yeah, they weren't the usual blasé L.A. bastards. Must be a fair number of out-of-towners out there," opines Shmucker.

"Are you kidding?" I counter. "Did you see the silicone?"

"Eh, maybe you're right. Maybe the tide's turning—comedy's on the upswing again."

"Fuckin' hope so—I've three more weeks of this. Where am I tomorrow?"

"Cleveland."

I wince. "Tomorrow night?"

"BP, for Christ's sake, do you ever look at your itinerary?"

"Not much. I love the uncertainty."

It's Shmucker's turn to wince. "You got tomorrow off," he states flatly in his Brooklynese whine. "You're flying to Cleveland tomorrow—I know, I know, routing's stupid, but the room's booked *solid* for the month and we *have* to do Cleveland and Leno's topping the bill—so sue me—and you get to hang in that wonderful City of Light for the whole evening *and* the next day, and you work the Crackerjack that night. Got it?"

Shmucker leads me to the dressing room, where a couple of paper cups containing Methode Champanoise sit bubbling under the makeup lights along with half-eaten veggies and fruit. Two wigs sit amongst the clutter, one blond, one brunette, left there by Caseload, who sometimes does a Female-Impersonator-Catatonic-on-Prozac routine but has obviously decided against it tonight.

I plop the blond wig on my head and pout into the mirror.

"What yer reckon, Perry? The English love this shit—did you mention tootski?"

"But the Americans don't," says Shmucker, removing the wig and dropping it in a bowl of salsa. "What about tootski?"

"I've been in the States a week with nary an intoxicant apart from a few hits of Vermont hydro-bud some chick in Portland hit me up with the other day. C'mon, I've been a good boy, this is your fucking town, Perry. What am I supposed to do, go back to the Hyatt bar and get drunk watching Skip E. Lowe do his thing?"

"I'll make a call," says Perry, his nose getting hungry.

Which he does on his black cellular as we cruise down the Strip in his black BMW toward the Sniper Room, with a stop on the way at an alfalfa 'n' avocado joint where Perry shoots in to cop the aforementioned substance from a waiter.

Next morning, I wake up in the Hyatt, the traffic drone outside making me feel as though my room is hanging directly over Sunset Boulevard. As I reach over to grab the other pillow with the express idea of bending it around my head to black out the endless car racket and the brightening sun as it cuts through the smog, I grasp not a pillow, but a head—a female head. Red, to be precise. Youch! The coke 'n' vodka hangover hits me like a wet rubber mallet and I remember staggering out of the Sniper, some chick on my arm whose name I don't recall right now, bringing her back to my room and somehow managing to bang her—unfortunately, as my memory retreads itself like a truck tire, without a fucking rubber!

Idiot! I leap out of bed and rush to the bathroom, where I check my privates for a sign that says, "You now have a *disease,* shithead!" But there's just this limp tool hanging there, slightly red and swollen around the rim, begging to have a grimace painted on it in scarlet lipstick, or perhaps a dunce's cap sewn into its blue veins to remind me that comedy is not a twenty-four-hour feeling.


Later that night, sitting in the sports bar of Cleveland's Grand Hotel, inches away from downtown, I pick at some onion rings and a burger and try to ignore the white-ass cookie-cutter drones who wander in and out yelling camaraderie-type remarks at each other as they gradually get shitfaced on large amounts of piss-flavored American beer. They're in town for some convention—plastics, concrete, computers, pesticides . . . whatever.

Soon enough, some platter-faced twentysomething fella starts bending his blocky head at me as I guzzle a glass of white wine and I know the Australian bit's coming (damn that Crocodile Dundee!). Right off the bat he says, "Where you from, buddy? Don't tell me . . . Australia!" Seeing as I've got nothing better to do, I try to explain to the oaf, whose brows are furrowing with incomprehension, the vast differences between the two nations, noting that I am, in fact, English. "We invented the language," I add with a dash of snideness.

A football game is on the TV and the name tags grab pitchers of swill and swing off to lonely circular tables. My new companion introduces himself as Tad or Chad or Bill and asks me what I "do," as if we've known each other for years. Usually, my standard reply to such familiarity is, "I'm a cocaine smuggler," which generally shuts the forward little bastards right up. But seeing as I still have half a gram in my wallet, which I am trying very hard to resist until after the show tomorrow night when I will be so depressed at the poor reaction that I will sorely need it, I opt for the truth instead and tell Chad that I'm a comedian, in town for an engagement at the Crackerjack tomorrow night, and would he like me to put his name on the door? Briefly,

Chad's eyes narrow as he inspects me more closely, but he is a maudlin drinker and remains unimpressed. Which is fine by me—less questions.

He does, however, drag me into a game of pool, challenging two older guys with different-coloured name tags—dangerous farming machinery reps, by the sound of it. He and I hunker around the blue baize with our sticks, assuming various manly, phallic postures, but get beaten on the eight ball anyway. Tad slaps his quarters down for the challenge match and halfway through the game, as I approach the table after much chalking of the cue tip and angle-assessing, he steps in front of me and stage-whispers, "Okay, Bob"—as in Bob Hope, the comedian—geddit?—"let's whup their asses!" Which we do, but we lose on the rubber. Eventually Bill gets swallowed up by his own colour-coded name tags and I manage to slope out of there to my room with a large glass of Chateau Ordinaire for a knockout drop. I have been through this same scenario so many times that I can no longer glean one speck of material from it. Not a one.

Next morning, nine-thirty, I'm pounding out of the hotel lobby in my mismatched jogging gear with a Conan O'Brian baseball cap on my unwashed hair and a little kangaroo change-holder Velcro-strapped around my wrist. I jog off, lurching through the chilly March air into downtown Cleveland.

I don't take in the street names but trust my sense of

direction, preferring to focus on the characters who inhabit the A.M. Within minutes, I'm running through a rundown section of town, past a Woolworth's, some hero joints, mom-and-pop pharmacies, and record stores. My pace picks up as I notice that there isn't a white face in sight. The inner-city blacks look aggrieved, hostile, either in a tired, beaten way, if they're older, or in an aggressive, threatening manner if they're young.

Last night on the news, from my comfortable hotel bed, I saw a clip on TV: some black guy named Rodney King was getting the shit beaten out of him by five or six white thugs masquerading as officers of the law. The racial tension triggered by this clip of amateur footage is reverberating around the country this very morning; I can feel it as sure as shit in the crisp morning air of downtown Cleveland. I veer right on a cross street, then head back toward the wider main drag with its safer vistas of big department stores and occasional white faces.

Jogging by one such department store, a most peculiar sight catches my eye. I slow down, backpedaling to the revolving doors to make sure I'm seeing what I think I'm seeing. Hopping weakly up and down, inches from the spinning doors that a customer laden with shopping bags has just exited, is what appears to be one of those battery-operated toys that street peddlers seem to be hawking everywhere these days. Only it's not a car with big tires that can hit an object and roll over and keep on going until it hits something else; and it's not one of those big-eyed puppy dogs that walk, stop, and flip over. It's a bird. I recognize it—from my youth as an amateur ornithologist—as a woodcock.

Bobbing is what the bird is doing, as if injured. As people come and go through the glass revolving doors, I lurch forward and pick the thing up, a clear sense arriving in my oxygenated brain that the creature is real. I've got the little fella in my hands; it nestles warmly, its tiny heart aflutter, its beady red eyes staring, stunned, at nothing much at all. Handsome black and chestnut bars stripe the upper half of its plumage, and striations of brown adorn a base of buff below. The woodcock's beak is long and pointy under a high forehead sporting the densest of its black stripes. It's about a foot or so long—about the size of a blue jay—but seems smaller in my hands, more air than solidity.

I'm standing there puffing, marveling at what I have in my hands, in downtown Cleveland. The woodcock is, in the U.K. at least, a game bird. You'll see paintings at the Tate Gallery of those grim English country kitchens with carcasses of hare, rabbit, pheasant, snipe, curlew, mallard (swan even!), and woodcock—anything the gentry can blow out of the sky that the cook can serve for dinner. But I had no idea that woodcock inhabited the States.

People are slowing down as they pass me to enter or exit the department store, glancing suspiciously at this nut who's standing dead still, staring at a fluffy ball with a beak like a stiletto.

I gently check the bird's anatomy for damage, starting with the crown, the forehead, and the iris, then on to the upper and lower mandibles of that impressive bill. The head area seems okay, which is a good sign. No blood appears to be oozing from its beak. I spread a wing, examining the lesser, median, and greater coverts, then move my fingers down to the secondaries and primaries, but nothing seems broken.

Two old ladies carrying packages exit the glass doors and ask me what it is I've got. I tell them, and one lady says, "You're a very nice young man," which makes me feel happy.

I'm now on a Save the Woodcock Mission and walk off, bird in hand, to find the nearest phone. As I bend against the increasing wind along the massive, windowless concrete wall at the side of the department building, two young black dudes in requisite baggy gear and shifty eyes lope up behind me.

"Wassat you got there?" demands one of them, and suddenly on this small section of an otherwise busy thoroughfare, there's just me, the woodcock, and two threatening-looking blacks the day after the Rodney King beating.

"Zat a woodpecker?" he asks, motioning at the bird with a jerky finger.

"It's a woodcock," I say, sharpening my pace a little. "I'm gonna try to call someone — a bird expert, the zoo . . . someone who'll know what to do. It's blown off-course," I add in an authoritative voice, as if I'm very much in control.

"A woodwhat?" questions the dude.

"A woodcock," I answer, turning to show them. Surely, I'm thinking, they won't mug a man with a woodcock in his hand?

"See the long bill? They use that to probe for worms in the mud. They're game birds," I explain, watching their faces as they squint at the ball of fluff in my hands. As I turn to walk away, the one who's been doing the talking says, "That's a good thing you're doin' there, brother." I turn and nod, almost tearing up with emotion.

One minute I'm convinced I'm about to meet an increasingly common — according to the popular news — tourist's demise, and the next I feel like the world really is just a great big onion or a bowl of cherries or a beautiful melting pot. Just as suddenly, I feel sad and lonely, and I want to be at my parents' house in the desolate English suburbs, drinking tea and eating chocolate biscuits, and I don't want to lead this lonely life anymore. Oh yes, and I want to hug everyone.

The dudes peel away like ragged crows, their baggy rayon jackets flapping in the wind. With a warmer heart, I step into a phone booth, where, after calls to various dog pounds and pet stores, I latch on to the biology department of the National Science Museum and find myself in conversation with the city's numero uno bird expert, whose name, appropriately enough, is Dr. John Byrd.

"You're at the Grand?" asks Byrd, whose specs and thinning hair I can visualize from my vantage point in the phone booth. "What's your name again?"

"Porker."

"The comedian?"

"You've heard of me?"

"My wife has your tape, *Live from the Lion's Den, Newcastle.*"

"No shit."

"Very funny."

"Thanks, Doctor . . ."

"Oh please, call me 'Birdman'—everyone does. Look, I'll get to the lobby in an hour. Get a bellhop to find a cardboard box and put the bird in it—just have someone hold it there. You don't have to hang around if you're busy."

"No, no, I've got nothing to do, er . . . Birdman. See you there."

And so with the woodcock quietly crouching in a cardboard box that once had contained a certain French red wine that would have married nicely with this particular game bird's tender, marinated, roasted flesh, I await the Birdman in the lobby of the Grand Hotel.

He arrives on time, his Danny Kaye–like nose entering the lobby first, closely followed by his tortoiseshell specs. My visualization turns out, cliché though it is, to be bang-on, with the exception of hair colour. I had imagined it as brown, but the Birdman's hair turns out to be yellowish, though thinning nonetheless. It hangs in lank strands of that pickled, formaldehyde shade that you might expect to see in a cancer patient about to expire.

Typical of ornithologists, entomologists, and all the hunched-over 'ologists the world over, his body seems a

217

good two feet behind his head, as if he is perpetually saying, "Here's my head, the rest of me will arrive shortly."

"Hi, I'm Brian," I say, carefully maneuvering my hand toward one of his uncoordinated limbs, which form gangly pincers around a pair of industrial-sized binoculars that hang on a mighty plastic cord around his neck and bounce off his sunken chest. He wears corduroy trousers and jacket, but of slightly different hues, and, incongruously, a pair of battered white Nikes where surely brown Oxford brogues should be.

"Birdman," says Dr. Byrd, by way of introduction.

We stare at the quiet bird in the wine box.

"Woodcock," announces the Birdman, and he picks the little fella up and performs a quick, skillful examination. "He looks all right. He should make it. So you're a bit of a 'twitcher' yourself, then, eh?"

"Twit . . . ?"

"Twitcher. Birder—one who spots birds to the point of obsession," the Birdman clarifies.

"Well, you know—used to be when I was younger. I thought it was a woodcock. What's it doing in the middle of Cleveland?"

"Happens all the time. They're migrating. They see the lights of the city, become confused, and fly into the windows. Heading north, you see."

"Ah."

"Here, can we leave him with the concierge for a moment? I want to show you something."

We leave Woody in his box, where he is beginning to flutter a bit, getting his senses back together. The valet promises to keep him safe behind his podium. The Birdman and I exit the lobby just as a crowd arrives all dressed in white for a wedding reception, which I see is taking place down the hall in a large conference room.

"Now take these," says the Birdman, handing me the giant binoculars, which feel like two garbage receptacles welded together, "and look up at that bird sitting on the ledge."

"You mean the pigeon?" I ask, finally focusing on a dull grayish creature that sits, face to a window, twenty-something floors up on the insurance building that adjoins the hotel.

"Ah, wait till its head turns," says the Birdman gleefully.

I stand there shivering, trying to keep the massive lenses steady, my arms already beginning to ache. Finally, the bird turns its head and I see the unmistakable hooked bill and pitiless eye of a raptor.

"What the . . ." I gasp. "What is it?"

"Peregrine," states the Birdman flatly.

"A peregrine falcon?"

"The other one's probably off hunting pigeons. Their feeding ground is the whole of downtown Cleveland. There's another pair that nest under a bridge by the stadium."

"Jesus!"

The peregrine shuffles up on the thin ledge of the insurance building but does not take flight. It just sits there, pigeonlike, with no hint of the awesome dynamics it would display in the hunt.

"Were they introduced?" I ask the Birdman, who does indeed appear to be twitching a little without the trusty binoculars in his hands.

"Yeah. They're doing okay, but we lost a pair last year. Toxins, we think."

"I'd love to see one hit a pigeon," I murmur, handing the lenses back before my neck seizes up.

"If you can stay another day, we could watch them. You might see a kill," offers the Birdman enthusiastically. People are walking by us; some look up, but without binoculars and a clear view of that beak, the falcon looks like a pigeon and their glances then turn questioningly to us.

I shake my head. "Nah, I'm off to St. Louis or somewhere tomorrow." I check my watch, thinking about a warm hotel room and a spot of work on my gags. "What about the woodcock?"

"Take it to some wasteland near Lake Erie and let it go, he should do all right. I've got to get back to NSM — I'm doing an autopsy on a swan this afternoon."

The Birdman asks me to put his name on the door plus one for tonight's gig, gives me some vague directions, and then lurches off, head leading the rest of him to his swan autopsy.

———

The wind is kicking up the garbage, sending plastic bags and scraps of paper whirling in micro-twisters as I walk at a goodly pace, woodcock in wine box, toward Lake Erie. There's a joke here somewhere, but I just can't seem to get at it.

The Birdman has directed me up Seventy-ninth Street across Chester and Superior avenues. With a red nose and numbing hands, I find myself under the steel girders of what may be the Cleveland Memorial Shoreway. Through the blackness of the giant black steel stanchions I can see the grey, horizonless vista of the lake. Menacing laughter echoes under the causeway and I notice three black kids kicking shit around. There are large cardboard boxes to my right; my pace quickens when I see one move in a way that suggests human habitation. Up above, traffic thunders east and west.

Once out of the darkness of the overpass, I move speedily, realizing I've got to retread that dank gauntlet before dark. Throwing fitful glances left and right, I become paranoid, expecting an ambush.

The light over the waste ground leading to the lake's shore is barely less threatening than the blackness under the elevated Shoreway, illuminating what looks like a hundred years of junk, like some sci-fi movie set of the blasted, nuclear-shocked future. The wind from the lake — which I can no longer see as the wasteland rises and falls in filthy, sandy hills before me — is charging in vicious gusts, now strong, now still, as if switches are being thrown by the wind gods.

I hunker down in the garbage between what once must have been ecologic sand dunes. Out of a pile of refuse resembling filthy white sheets and underwear that appears to have been ripped to shreds by a maniac and stuffed in various car parts and oil drums, a large, bristly Norway rat pops up and makes a beeline for a similar pile of junk, its obscene, pinkish tail bouncing like an intestine behind it.

"What the fuck am I doing here?" I enunciate quietly, and my words sound very puny.

As I open the box with blueing fingers, the woodcock starts, then crouches, as if it knows this damn fool human is doing it no favours by releasing it here. But it does not struggle as I lift it to the wind, where it fidgets in anticipation of its freedom.

I stand up and stare silently for a moment at the roiling grey cloud bank covering the lake, grasping the bird with my right hand. Just as I am about to release it, I hear a groaning sound. With a growing sense of unease, I realize it is a human sound.

I spin around, expecting the three black youths and any number of knives and guns, but there is a white guy standing there, cold blueish lips hanging limp below a pair of sweaty-looking rheumy eyes that don't seem to go with the lips at all. He's just standing there, as if he just dropped out of the grey canopy above. Beyond him, I can see the Cleveland Memorial Shoreway, studded with speeding vehicles.

The man's brown, matted hair clings in strands around

his face, Manson-like, and his colourless pants and ripped, once-white shirt flap in the wind. He faces me for another moment, then lurches forward in a threatening manner.

He is merely feet away and I can't take my eyes from his as I instinctively raise my right hand with the only weapon I have, plunging it at the bastard's wayward right eyeball, pulling short of my target at the last moment.

Out of his blue lips and jagged, yellowing teeth come a surprised yelp, almost sober-sounding. It registers that somewhere under the surface of poverty and abuse this guy is probably only in his late twenties.

He staggers backwards, trying to focus. His gaze fixes on the woodcock, which has remained steadfast and calm throughout the whole ordeal. The bum, judging by his total bafflement, cannot put it together in his alky/cracked-out brain: it's like he sees it, but can't grasp the fact that I have just threatened to deal him a fell blow with a game bird.

Backwards he goes, reeling, miraculously not tripping ass-over-tit on the jagged heaps of refuse. His hand moves mechanically to his face. Then he appears to examine his fingers, as if he really has been stabbed. A look of horror contorts his features, like he's hallucinating liquid eyeball material on his hand.

I stand there watching the chump spinning back in a panic toward the cardboard villages under the causeway until he disappears, bellowing into the blackness. The three black youths I had noticed earlier materialize, hovering uncertainly between the dunes and the dark shelter of the suspended road. They stare back and forth between me and the tramp.

I raise the woodcock to the wind, hoping to Christ its neck isn't broken and that this triumphant scenario will not be dashed by the specter of a limp bird carcass dropping to the cold ground. As the creature is lifted skyward, my audience of three looks on dumbfounded. I holler "Go!" and release the little fella into a strong gust of wind, which he takes without hesitation, and whirls upwards toward the Cleveland Memorial Shoreway, up into the grey sky toward the city, heading for the soft muddy marshlands of the south. South, I realize with mild disappointment, is the wrong way.

What happens next, however, replaces my slight deflation at the bird's error of judgment with a deep shock. From the tumbling clouds, a grey scimitar of black-eyed fury ascends like a flint arrowhead, aiming straight for the woodcock.

"So you saw one of our peregrines make a hit, eh?" The Birdman is backstage, just before I go on.

"Oh, man!" I exclaim. "You should have seen it, Birdman. Just when I thought it was gonna take the woodcock, it veers off under the Shoreway and whacks a pidgeon, pow!"

The applause for the last act is dying down. I drag in lungfuls of air, steadying my nerves. "Go out there and get a seat," I urge the Birdman. "There's only about a hundred and fifty empty ones!"

"Good luck, Brian!"


The relentlessly tasteless decor of the Crackerjack Comedy Club negates any chance of a conducive atmosphere that might be created by a successful gag; but the audience — all forty-eight of them in the two-hundred-seater — attempt gamely to conjure some warmth between the uneven black walls.

My joke about the queer Scottish pedophile doing a turn at his local pub on Hogmanay ("Luck Be a Laddie," "Laddie Be Good," "Once, Twice, Three Times a Laddie," and "Who's That Laddie?" are part of his repertoire) appears to be incomprehensible to the Clevelanders. I have more luck with off-the-cuff quickies: "Guy goes to a doctor and says, 'Doctor, I've got a bit of a problem: I have five penises.' 'Tell me,' says the doctor, 'how do your underpants fit?' 'Like a glove' " — that sort of thing.

But I'm going for the long, complex Native American customs officials gag regardless. I plow into it, checking the Birdman, his wife, and the name-tag guy from the hotel bar for their reactions. Name Tag, however, is no barometer, seeing as his every half-arsed response appears three or four seconds behind everybody else's. He's sitting near the back of the room, alone, with three empty tables dotted around him. The place would have been packed if Leno, who was scheduled to appear, hadn't canceled after he drove one of his antique steam-powered automobiles off a cliff in L.A. and fractured his jaw. As it is, the other four acts on the bill are third-stringers like myself—not much to tempt the punters away from the sports bars, Hooters, or their TV sets, really.

Thank God for the Birdman's wife, I think. She is a tiny, sparrowlike woman with dull plumage, but she has a laugh like a stevedore and her darkling *Passer domesticus domesticus* eyes are teary with mirth. Her gaiety is infectious, and the crowd gets behind the Native American sketch full tilt. I hit the home stretch, all cylinders firing, and score big-time with a rousing roar.

Backstage, though, before the second glass of Methode Champanoise and the fat line in the toilet kick in, I think, as I often do, about quitting. I think about the Birdman, wishing I'd had a better education and had studied biology, ornithology, and a few other 'ologies at some posh university. I wish I'd taken my wit and intelligence seriously as a kid and fought my way through the English class-structured education system to become something. How many jokes can you tell? How many third-full houses can you play to? How many airports and name-tag morons do you have to deal with? How many fucking hotel rooms do you need to become depressed in before you hang yourself from a lighting fixture? And for what?

This feeling evaporates as the drink and coke induce their rosy, self-congratulatory glow. In comes the Birdman and his wife, with Lena Strange, the last act on the bill tonight. The three of them are all smiles and victory, making a fuss about the Native American customs officials. And tomorrow? I'm off to St. Louis and then God knows where else Perry Shmucker's got me booked, before the last leg, which takes in the Catskills and down to Virginia—whatever. Should be a barrel of laughs.